Your Dimension or Mine?

by

Cynthia Kimball

The Dating Service Series

Your Dimension or Mine?

COPYRIGHT © 2014 by Cynthia Kimball

Cover Art by *Tamra Westberry*

The Wild Rose Press, Inc.
PO Box 708
Adams Basin, NY 14410-0708
Visit us at www.thewildrosepress.com

Publishing History
First Faery Rose Edition, 2014
Print ISBN 978-1-62830-239-4
Digital ISBN 978-1-62830-240-0

The Dating Service Series
Published in the United States of America

"Yep. Chocolate can be used in all sorts of food. This"—she grabbed the cake—"is the one I talked about in my email." After taking the closest utensil and filling it with the warm, gooey center, she handed him the spoon.

The moment the food hit his tongue, she knew he loved it. His eyes closed and a small moan left his throat. "That is divine. There is nothing like it on my planet. What does it come from?"

"A plant on Earth. I know there is a lot they have to do to the cacao bean to make it into chocolate, but whatever they do, it is so worth it."

They talked and laughed their way through the tremendous amount of chocolate. The only thing he wasn't sold on was the bowl of chocolate-flavored cereal, but that was fine with her. She ate them all. As the last plate was cleared and she leaned back, basking in the sun—it might not be as harsh as the Arizona heat, but it was still nice—a shadow crossed over her. She looked up at Terrian who was staring intently at her mouth. "What?"

"There is a spot of chocolate you missed," he said, his voice taking on a tone that made her heart beat a little faster.

"Can you get it off?" she asked a little more breathily than she would have liked.

He leaned in and his lips softly touched the left corner of her mouth, his tongue sliding softly over her skin. There was a pause and then he kissed her again, this time, his lips slid a little further over hers. His soft lips were like velvet, and with a sigh, she wrapped her arms around his neck as she kissed him back.

Praise for Cynthia Kimball's writings

"A feel-good, happy-ending story for those who believe in that and need to read it once in a while. I couldn't stop smiling the entire time I was reading it, and I look forward to the next few times I read it."

~*~

"I like being led down the path of exploration into a whole other way of finding a soul mate. The twists and turns of trusting what one wants... even if you think you are doing so to shush another. Great tale, wonderful spin on a new idea in finding love!"

~5 stars

~*~

"It's a good read when I feel like I have returned from a journey rather than finished a story."

~5 stars

~*~

"Bursting at the seams with great characters..."

~*~

"There's a real kinetic sense to this, both in terms of the narrative and the ideas."

~5 Stars

Dedication

To those who believe there is more out there
than just dust particles, I dedicate this novel.
After all, who's to say there aren't different dimensions,
and your perfect mate
might just happen to be in one of them.

Chapter One - *A Jane-Approved Date*

"...and of course there is the effect on the economy..."

Sighing, Ari blinked her eyes and stared at the man seated directly across from her. He was still talking. And eating. From the moment they were seated at the private table for two in the neighborhood's newest restaurant, Jay had been stuffing his face. Or talking. Sometimes he attempted multi-tasking and did them both at the same time. When that happened, Ari wanted to ask their waiter for a splatter guard but worried it would come across as rude.

"These damned politicians just don't know anything," he finished his newest rant, taking a big gulp of wine before letting out a belch.

If only Ma Nature would choose this moment to send a tsunami our way, she thought. Of course, the possibility of that happening was less than zero. The closest they got were flash floods in August. It was January.

"Have you noticed the price of gas?" Jay asked, munching on a breadstick as the waiter removed his salad plate and replaced it with a large bowl of soup. Without waiting for her to acknowledge his question, he launched into a diatribe about fixing prices and the state of pigs...or at least that was what she thought he said.

Letting her mind drift, Ari tried to remember why she accepted this date in the first place. Oh, that's right—her sister Jane set it up without asking. Well, it wasn't the first time. Ever since she entered college, Jane had taken it upon herself to introduce her little sister to men just like her husband Tony.

First, Jane set her up with Sebastian. The main thing Ari remembered about him was he looked like Rambo and giggled like a girl when someone passed gas. Then there was Erin, though he went by Igor. He had an unnatural obsession with Frankenstein even going so far as to take upon himself the appearance of a prometheus—neckbolts and all—to prove whatever point he was trying to make. Ari did not care enough to find out what that point was.

The waiter removed Jay's empty soup bowl and placed each of their dinner plates in front of them. Ari might have been seeing things, but it seemed as though the boy in black trousers and a crisp white shirt glanced at her pityingly.

Looking at her plate, she was pleased to find the meal on the smallish side. Maybe if she was lucky, the date would end soon. She glanced up at Jay, noting the rate he was eating.

She took a couple bites, relieved when he started talking again so she could go back to ruminating. Her mind went back to her catalogued list of Jane-approved, Ari-disgruntled men. After Igor, she had been set up with gary. That's right, he spelled his name lowercase. Then Paul and Steve—all sports enthusiasts with a combined IQ of the University of Arizona's wins for the season.

For two years after college graduation, while she

was getting her master's degree in library science, things were quiet because Jane was too busy taking care of seven children, including three babies. The moment she got her master's degree and got a job at the University of Arizona Library, the dates started up again. She was never asked to go on a date. Instead, she received an email with a place and time, as well as a list of acceptable outfits.

Pierce, the yeah-man, was her first post-graduate date. After every sentence, he would add the phrase, "yeah, man." Then there was Devon, the sanctimonious I-work-for-God-so-you-are-so-lucky preacher dude. And now, Jay.

Wait. Of course, there was also Edward.

When Jane first told Ari about Edward, she had just read the Twilight series and visualized a tall, pale, sexy redhead. Unfortunately, Edward turned out to be short with a beer gut who also punctuated each of his phrases with an eyebrow wiggle and pelvic thrust. She had not been able to read Twilight since.

"So, Arrrrwin," Jay said, growling the 'r' like a pirate while pronouncing her given name wrong. Against her better judgment, she tuned back into the conversation. "Jane tells me you were a bit crazy in college." He winked at her and leered.

As she fought back the food threatening to come back up her esophagus, she caught the look of pity from a woman one table over. Obviously, Jay's voice carried. Taking a deep staggering breath, she sat up straight. What had Jane told him? "Aren't all college students?" she hedged.

He chuckled, shoving the last of his linguini with clam sauce into his mouth. Her stomach heaved at the sight, and she started mentally repeating the phrase "It will soon be over" to herself.

The phrase stopped when he added, "Yeah, but most coeds don't write and produce their own—"

Whatever he was going to say was stopped as the sounds of a non-musically inclined singer came from his pocket. To Ari's surprise and amusement, he blushed and stammered, "I-I'll be right back. Have to take this."

He jumped out of his seat and ran out of the restaurant, walking around to the glass side of the building where he talked on the phone while finger combing through his almost thinning brown hair in the glass—seemingly unaware he could be seen from the other side when he picked his nose. Snickering at how stupid he looked, Ari wondered what he had been about to say. What would Jane have told him?

Unconsciously, her eyes fell to his lips. As a child she had such bad ear infections that hearing went from difficult to near impossible, so she had learned to lip read. For the next five minutes she ate her meal, her eyes flipping to his lips every so often to see if he was done yet. After swallowing the last piece of chicken on her plate, she looked up and as her mind made a connection with the words formed by his lips, she slowly set her fork down. Well, now she had an apt description for the newest Jane-approved loser.

"Are you okay?" The woman from the next table leaned forward with a mixture of concern and interest on her face. She probably thought this would be a fun thing to relay to all her friends. Ari figured her expression must look as murderous as she currently felt.

"Fine," she lied with a well-practiced smile. "Blind

date."

Nodding, while not able to hide her disappointment that there was no gossip to be had, the woman turned back to her food. Less than a minute later, Jay sat back down.

"Sorry about that," he said with a smirk. Objectively, Ari wondered how he could call the woman on the phone "sweetie", "honey", and "love" one moment and look down her cleavage the next. With the lower-than-average intelligence of the men she had dated, added to this newest of lows, Ari began to wonder if any man was worth dating, let alone anything else. "What were we talking about?"

Part of her wanted to just walk out, but curiosity kept her in her seat. Okay, she thought, we'll play this game a little longer. "You were mentioning what Jane told you about me...in college," she added at his blank expression.

The blank look left, the leer returned, and his eyes fastened on her chest. "Yeah, she told me that..." He lowered his voice and leaned across the table so far he was practically in her face. His breath reeked of garlic and the fake mint used in breath mints. Ari leaned back as far as she could without actually tipping the chair legs. "You made adult films."

Mouth dropping open, she stared at him unblinkingly. "What?" she squeaked after a few seconds, fully aware of how understated that reaction was.

Snickering, he sat back, finally giving her room to breathe. "Yep. I was not about to turn down the chance to date a porn star. I know what you *ladies* can do." The inflection in his voice when he said the word ladies made her skin prickle, and she finally understood the phrase *it can make your skin crawl.*

Rubbing her palms furiously over her upper arms, trying to get rid of the feeling, she looked everywhere but at the man across the table. Porn? Adult films? There had to be a misunderstanding. Maybe the Jay she was supposed to meet got there late, and she ended up with the wrong one. "I think you have the wrong girl," she started to say.

He chuckled again. "Are you saying *The Widow's Revenge* and *Take it All* aren't yours? Jane told me about them." Leaning back, he continued to leer as the waiter removed their plates.

"Would you like anything else?" the waiter asked quietly, looking between the two of them.

"Check please," she said quickly, not sure if she should burst out laughing or run from the room. She chose the third option females the world over had used for centuries. "I'll be right back." Standing up, she walked quickly to the women's restroom and locked herself inside.

"Oh my," she sighed at the aghast expression on her face. Pulling out her phone, she called the one person who would get the irony, her eldest sister Cory.

"Hey, little sister, aren't you supposed to be on a date?" Cory's snicker on the last word helped her relax.

"You will not believe what she set me up with!"

"Oh yes, I would. What's the problem with this one?"

Cory was more likely to be on Ari's side and always had been. Not only was she twenty years older, so she was more like an aunt than a big sister, but when it came to men she understood the issues. Well,

6

considering she was born one, she understood them more than any woman Ari knew. In fact, if Cory ever set her up on a date, it would probably be spot on, but so far she hadn't tried.

"You mean besides the fact he continually feeds his face, talks while he eats, and is married?"

"Married?" Cory shrieked. "What the hell is Jane doing setting you up with a married man?"

"I don't try to understand the workings of Jane's mind," Ari moaned. "But, sis, she also told him I made adult films in college."

"Uh…hold on, I'm getting her on the line."

As Ari waited to be connected, she rolled her eyes at the knock at the door. "Occupied!" Hopefully, whoever it was didn't have to go real bad, because she wasn't sure how long this would take.

"Okay, we all here?" Cory piped in.

"Yep!"

"I'm here too," Ari added with frustration.

"Arwen, why are you on the phone with Cory? Aren't you on a date with Jay?"

Ari ground her teeth together. She hated it when Jane used her given name, especially in that condescending tone.

Cory chuckled. "That seems to be the problem, Jane. Not only have you set her up with another winner"—Jane huffed—"this one is married, and he seems to think she's in the porn industry."

Ari expected Jane to scoff and scold her, once again, for not appreciating her efforts. She did not expect her to start giggling.

While she waited for Jane to get hold of herself, another knock came at the door. "Still occupied! Don't know how long I'll be!"

"First, he's not married," Jane said calmly once she could speak, "though he does have an on-again, off-again girlfriend. Second," she giggled again, "you know Tony refers to those movies you made as adult films. Jay's eyes lit up and I was not about to burst his bubble. He was salivating to meet you."

"Jane!" Ari felt a mixture of exasperation and anger at her sister as well as the desire to burst out laughing at the misguided idiot sitting out in the restaurant. "Those were mini-documentaries I wrote and produced on the reproductive processes of insects! They were not porn films!" She practically screeched at the end to stop herself from laughing.

Wincing at how loud her voice had become, she quieted down. "Look Jane, that's it. I am not going on another date you set me up on. Period!"

A long beleaguered sigh poured through the phone making her gut clench. "You are over-reacting, Ari. You bury yourself in that library of yours. If it weren't for me, you would never date and you know it."

The all-too-familiar sinking sensation started in her stomach, and the guilt was not far behind. Jane was a master at laying on guilt. Ari was so focused on her own body, she wasn't sure how to respond. Luckily, Cory came to her rescue.

"That's cold, Jane. Ari isn't like you. She can have a life without a man in it."

Ouch! That was not making her feel better. What happened to Cory the rescuer?

"I'm not going to stop setting her up!"

Ari rubbed her temples as her two sisters bickered back and forth about who had Ari's best interests at heart. Finally, she couldn't take it anymore.

"Could you at least set me up with someone intelligent?"

"Devon was intelligent," Jane countered without missing a beat.

Groaning, Ari leaned against the sink. She could not believe they were having this discussion in the bathroom of a restaurant. "Look, I've got to go end this date, Jane. This is not the end of this discussion. We do not have the same taste in men."

A few more whines from Jane and some interfering from Cory, and she shoved the phone in her pocket. Looking into the mirror, she straightened her shirt and plastered on a fake smile. "Time to end this date."

Opening the door, she strode back to the table where Jay was noticeable by his absence. When she reached her chair, she realized his suit coat and briefcase were missing as well. "Weird."

She had just taken her seat and was drumming her fingers on the table when the waiter walked up. This time there was no doubt as to the pity on his face. "The guy you were with had to leave and asked that I give this to you." He handed her a folded piece of paper.

Relieved she didn't have to do the leaving, she nodded, and opened up the paper to see what kind of excuse he would have left for his departure. Instead of a note, she found herself staring at the bill for their dinner. "So, he decided we were going dutch," she chuckled, grabbing her bag. Boy, her sister sure knew how to pick them.

"No, actually he said you would be paying for the whole bill."

Chapter Two - *The Discriminating Single*

Slamming her front door behind her, Arwen Maria Reynolds stomped across her linoleum floor, leaving a trail of water behind her. "There isn't supposed to be rain in February," she grumbled, pulling off her soaked tank top, dress pants, bra, and underwear the moment she reached her bathroom. Usually she was in a good mood on a Friday afternoon, especially the Friday afternoon before a three-day weekend. But not this Friday.

From the very beginning, it had been rife with stress. Some idiot had taken to putting religious leaflets between the pages of the books in the mystical section, and all available librarians, which of course she technically was since she did not work with the public, were called upon to find them all. Seven hours later, the books were finally sitting as they should be, instead of bursting at the seams. A pile of over a thousand pamphlets were strewn at her feet.

By the time she got back to her desk to finish inputting the newest serials for the week, the network was down, and three irate calls got her nowhere. Two nice lectures by her boss about being a team player later, she left the library only to find it raining a deluge outside. Of all days she chose to walk to work, it would be the one when it rained.

After taking a long hot shower that did not improve

her mood, she dried off, changed into her comfy terrycloth robe, and went in to the kitchen to heat up soup and some milk for hot chocolate. To end the Friday from hell, her sisters were coming over to talk with her about her "dating situation." When they discussed it on the phone about a week previous, Jane had said it so oddly that Ari could practically see her using hand quotes to punctuate her meaning.

Her soup was barely warm when the first knock came at her door. "Nooo," she whined like a little child, rolling her eyes at herself as she walked to the door. Before opening it however, she took a deep breath to calm herself. If she acted like a child, Jane would have the upper hand right away. Once she felt calm enough, she turned the handle. To her relief, Cory was there first. "Hey, sis."

Cory walked in, imposing at over six feet tall, and yet her reddish blonde hair that fell just over her shoulders and her soft blue eyes confirmed her kind heart. Ari was sure her sister could not hurt a fly. Well, not true. She had seen her kill many a fly, spider, scorpion, and any number of horrid insects. But that wasn't the point.

Since Jane hadn't gotten there yet, Ari relaxed and drank her soup and chocolate while Cory talked about her day. "Ready for tonight?" she asked once Ari was done.

"It's been an awful day. So I don't know how it could get worse. I am not going out with any more of her guys though." Ari grimaced at her own tone. Even she didn't believe her. True, she didn't want to go on any Jane-approved dates anymore, but she never had been one to fight for her rights. Especially against a sister who was a decade older and wielded guilt like a weapon. Their mother would have been so proud.

"Well, I think she is coming armed with ideas. So be prepared for a Jane attack."

Groaning, Ari went over to the cookie jar and carried it into the living room. "If I'm going to put up with that, I'm gonna do it with cookies."

She had just put the jar down on the coffee table when a series of loud raps came at the door, Jane's signature *soft, hard, soft, boom* knock. Ari opened the door, grimacing at her sister who was wrapped up in the kind of winter coat you only needed if you lived some place like Jackson Hole, Wyoming. Jane walked in, removed her coat, sweater, and galoshes, before walking into the living room, barely acknowledging her baby sister.

"Cory, how was your trip?" she asked, taking a cookie and sitting down in Ari's favorite chair. Her short white blonde hair was styled into a bob that she somehow kept tamed even with the humidity in the air. At only five-feet-two, she was the shortest of the sisters, yet somehow she was also the bossiest.

"Good. Got two more contracts signed so I'll be busy through the end of next year."

"And Brent?"

"Brent's doing fine. He is in Florida doing something for a theme park."

"Good, good." Jane turned her eyes to Ari. "And how is the library?"

Sighing, Ari flumped onto the sofa next to Cory and grabbed a couple cookies. "Good for the most part. The whole place was crazy today." She didn't feel like telling them about the pamphlets. Jane wasn't really in the mood to hear about it anyway.

"Well, we all know why we are here," Jane began.

Cory nodded. "So you can harp on Ari about the fact she doesn't date."

A snicker bubbled up Ari's throat, but she pushed it back.

"I don't harp," Jane snapped, her normal calm demeanor ruffled for a moment. "But Cory, you have to admit, Arwen is not any good at finding a date. And—"

"And," Cory cut in and Arwen began to wonder if she even needed to be here for the conversation. "You have taken Mom's last request a bit intensely and, in my opinion, the wrong way."

Pursing her lips, Jane took a bite of a cookie. "Mom asked that we make sure Ari was happily married."

"Exactly. And by happily, I take it to mean that she's with someone of her same intellect. You take it to mean someone you would be attracted to."

A faint blush lit Jane's cheeks. "What do you have against Tony?"

Chuckling, Cory grabbed a cookie. "Nothing. He's perfect for you. But Ari is nothing like you, Jane. The kind of person who would be perfect for her is not your type."

They continued to quibble back and forth, never once asking for Ari's input. Part of her felt annoyed about that, but the other part, the part that did not want to argue, was quite happy with the way things were working out. Until…

Jane turned to look at her. "So, what are you going to do about it?"

Gulping the last of her cookie, Ari shrugged. "I

don't see what's so wrong with focusing on my career. I'm only twenty-eight."

Her sister sighed. "I was married with four children by the time I was twenty-eight. Cory had three long-term relationships by that time. There is more to life than work, Arwen."

Chuckling, Cory stood up and walked into the kitchen. "You know, this kind of thing never would have happened to the real Arwen."

Ari laughed. "No, she had Aragorn to defend her."

Jane cracked a smile. "How did you get stuck with such a fanciful name? Cory was born Corren, which she changed to Corrine, and I was given the name Jane. But you…"

"Mom was reading *Fellowship of the Rings* when I was born. The last scene she read before they whisked her into the delivery room mentioned Arwen. I bet if I had been twins, the other would have been named Frodo."

"Or Frodette," Cory offered, coming back with three mugs of milk.

The conversation veered away from her dateless life for a while, and the three chatted like they normally would at their weekly get-togethers. Then Jane looked at her watch. "Oh! I need to get home. Tony has to be at work in an hour." She turned her eyes on Ari, a speculative gleam in her eye. "So, let's solve this little issue. I will grant that I never meet the kind of men you might fall for, but I will keep trying unless…"

Ari started groaning, but sat up straight at the last word. "Unless?"

"Watch it," Cory stage-whispered. "Jane has something up her sleeve."

"Unless you promise to go on one date a month." Jane stood up, satisfied, and drank the last of her milk before going into the kitchen and placing it in the sink.

"No way!"

Cory placed a hand on Ari's knee, stopping any further exclamations. "A date a month when she never dates? That's asking a lot, Jane. Even you don't set her up that often."

"So? If she wants me to stop setting her up, she will set herself up."

Ari sent Cory a "help" through lips that would not make a sound. She could not imagine trying to line up monthly dates. Didn't Jane get the memo? Arwen was clueless when it came to men. The few times she was actually around a guy she was attracted to, she lost all ability to think and came across as a ninny. This scenario had neurotic film written all over it. If they did it without clothes, Jay would be thrilled.

Standing up, Cory walked over and stood next to Jane. At an inch over six feet, she was almost a foot taller, thus giving her the semblance of control. "What if she does it a different way?"

"Meaning?" Jane asked, glancing at their little sister where she sat wrapped up in her terrycloth robe watching them with wide eyes.

"Online dates. There are tons of online dating sites. She could meet guys there, weed out the idiots, get to know the others…"

"Oh. Now that has promise," Jane nodded, her eyes starting to twinkle. "Five of my friends met their husbands online." Turning she grabbed a pen from Ari's pen jar. Their mother had a pen jar in every room when they were growing up, and all three women did

15

the same. It was one of their few homages to their mother. Walking back to her chair, she grabbed her purse, pulled out her notebook, and tore out a piece of paper. Scribbling something on it, she handed it to Ari.

"These are the sites my friends used. Join them. I will want weekly updates!"

Before Ari could agree or disagree, Jane was out the door.

Chuckling, Cory walked over and looked at the list. "Well-known sites. You might as well do it, Ari. This should keep Jane at bay, plus who knows, maybe you will meet someone."

Ari smiled to herself. Cory was always sure to use gender-neutral comments when referring to someone she might end up with, unsure of whether she was hetero or homosexual. Except for one crazy night in college, Ari definitely liked guys. But she appreciated her sister's thoughtfulness anyway.

"Okay, I will give it a try. It's better than another Jay—WAIT!" Ari rose and ran to the door, opening it and yelling, "Jane! You still owe me for that date!" Jane had promised to reimburse her the $42.49 for that horrible meal with Jay.

"Good luck with that," Cory chuckled, hugged her sister and left, running swiftly through the raindrops to her car.

Closing the door, Ari went back into the living room and grabbed the cookie jar, taking it back into the kitchen, where she placed it in its spot to the left of the oven. After stuffing the paper in the pocket of her robe, she washed the cups and placed them on the counter to dry. Then, after going back into the living room and curling up in her chair, she pulled out the list.

"Oops." Looking down she saw her pocket was wet. She must have leaned up against the counter. Now the letters on the paper were wiggly and out of focus. Some she could make out. Matchinone.com. Yes, she had heard of that one. OKdate. Sounded boring, but she could check it out. The third one though was hard to make out. The name was a blue blur, but the description next to it was somewhat legible. *for the… dimension…ability.*

Chuckling, she set the piece of paper by her computer and went to bed. There was plenty of time in the morning to set up a few online profiles to placate her crazy sister.

****

The next morning proved to be another rainy one. "Geez! Come on Ma Nature! It's winter!" Sighing, Ari pulled herself out of bed and went through her normal morning rituals, except she did not go running. Running down by the park was one of her favorite things to do. Just not in the rain. She was lucky she wasn't sick from walking home the day before, and she was not one to press her luck.

Without the run, her shower, breakfast, and running through the channels only to find nothing was on took a lot less time than normal. That left nothing to do except read or go on the computer. Glancing at the little piece of paper, she thought it would be a good time to get that out of the way and turned on her laptop.

In the time it took her to get a cup of hot cider, her computer was up and running and already notifying her she had new emails. Unsurprising, five were spam, and only one was something she wanted to look at. She ended up surfing through her favorite online shoe store before she remembered the whole online dating thing.

"Oh, right. Okay, let's see what this whole thing is about."

It turned out to be a lot more complicated than she expected. Just filling out a profile was a monumental task, and she had to do one for each site? This would take forever. Grumbling through each question, she forced herself through the Matchinone and OKdate profile screens. She uploaded the same photo on both, an image taken the year before when she and two other women from the library went to San Diego for Labor Day weekend. She looked at the photo critically. It wasn't the best photo she had ever taken, but she was smiling at least.

Ari wasn't one of those girls who looked down on their looks. She thought she was pretty enough, with her shoulder-length blonde hair and hazel eyes, though she didn't think that counted for much. She still didn't attract the right sort of men. After four hours of mind-numbing entries, she elected to do the other site later. She needed food.

The rest of the afternoon, she spent doing the simple things: grocery shopping, a wax job, getting a juice drink at the mall. After she got home and made her dinner, it was only six and with nothing else to do, she went back to the computer to create a profile at the unknown dating site. She considered calling Jane to ask but figured she would look up the description first. It made no sense to her, so she typed it into a search engine.

dating dimension ability

She received over thirty-four million responses of which the first real one was titled *Does Penis Size*

Really Matter? "Yes," she snickered conversationally as she looked through the results trying to find a dating site. Fourth and fifth down were two site listings for eCongruence, which sounded rather cheesy to her. As she went on to the second page of results, something on the right caught her eye.

Interdimensional Dating Service
For the discriminating single
Not for everyone

Interdimensional? Now that sounded like it might fit the bill! And they sounded snooty which Jane would correlate with upscale intellectual. Smiling because she had been able to find the site herself, she clicked the link and waited for it to load. To her surprise, the screen flickered three times before the site popped up. "Well that was weird." She looked out her front window, wondering if there was a power outage coming. It was not unheard of in her building.

The site was laid out rather simply, so she figured the profile questionnaire would not take as long as the others. Looking through their front page, she was amused at some of the usernames and pictures. The faces did not look quite right, as if they were slightly out of focus, but then the images were so tiny it was hard to see anything. And the usernames? On the other sites, she had seen usernames like *waiting4you* and *NeedUNow*. Here they seemed to want to be funny. One was called *DifferentiallyOrdinary* and another *CoordinationallyBlatant*. Maybe this site was more for people like her.

Humming to herself, she clicked the link that said *SignUp* and came to a regular information page. She filled in her email address, description, photo, as well as a small history about herself, and clicked to the next page. At the top, it read *3 of 12 pages*. "Twelve pages? Ewww." Well, she was already in, she should probably continue.

Deciding wine would help, she went into the kitchen and poured herself a glass of her favorite red, electing to bring the bottle back in with her, just in case. After taking a sip, she sighed and sat down. "Whoever decided to make a wine that has a hint of chocolate was brilliant." After taking two more large sips, she went back to the profile. The questions were worded strangely. She wondered if the site was created by someone for whom English was not their first language.

For if you had a choice, what hair on top of head would you like?

"I would prefer there would be hair," she chuckled aloud.

The question was multiple choice, and the answers were even more odd than the question.

Tough
Wiry
Cotton-ized
Shriveled
Bear

"This has got to be a joke." There was a microscopic picture next to each word, which gave her an indication of what they were talking about. Tough was short and straight, Wiry was sticking up, Cotton-ized looked like an afro, while Shriveled didn't make any sense whatsoever. Bear, however, meant bald. "Why didn't they use bare?" Maybe this wasn't for the intellectual. Finishing her wine, she poured another glass and, after marking *Tough*, went on to the next question.

What body type you prefer?
Two arm
Four arm
Two leg
Four leg
One head
Two head

A snort escaped her lips at the images. They showed a stick drawing of someone with four arms, four legs, and two heads. Chugging the rest of her wine, she ploughed on.

By the seventh page when enough alcohol infiltrated her system, the questions started to make sense.

Do you handle change well?

Yes, she marked quickly, unsure if it was the truth but too buzzed to care.

An interdimensional shift can cause mood swings. Would this bother you?

"No." She snickered as she clicked the button. No doubt the oddness of these questions was due to her drinking. Tomorrow when she woke up, they wouldn't be nearly as funny.

For over an hour, she answered their questions, laughing constantly. When the screen popped up *Complete,* she was almost disappointed. Feeling tipsy and yawning like crazy, she turned off her computer and went to bed. Maybe tomorrow the weather would be nice enough so she could run off the alcohol. That would work, she thought as she drifted into a sleep filled with men who had multiple arms, legs, and other appendages.

Chapter Three - *Interdimensional Dating Service*

Somebody was pounding on her head. Groaning, Ari tried to open her eyes only to find that her eyelids seemed sealed shut. Cautiously, she reached out with her left hand, trailing her fingers across soft cotton sheets. When they reached open air, she stretched further until coming into contact with a smooth surface. Letting her fingers continue, she ran up what she assumed was a leg until she reached the top of what was undoubtedly her side table. The moment her hand made contact with the shot glass Cory bought her the last time she went to Vegas, she knew where she was.

"I'm definitely in my own bed," she murmured, wincing as each word pounded against her brain. Ouch! Memories came to her, opaque and clouded with some sort of fog. Dating services. Wine…drunk…hangover.

Groaning again, she rolled over and buried her head into her pillow. Why had she drunk so much? She hadn't done that since the day she received her bachelor's degree. Now she was glad she had not been able to open her eyes. That was a level of pain she did not want to add to her already overwhelming headache.

Bam! Bam! Bam!

"Ow!" she yelped, accidentally opening her eyes, which made the pain so much worse. "No!" she cried as she closed them again. Why was someone pounding on her door at what must be an unreasonable hour?

The pounding continued until she crawled out of bed and made her way toward it. Using her hands to guide her, she finally found the door. Opening it with a jerk, she spat, "Stop that!"

"You look like hell." The amusement in her friend Denise's voice made her growl. "Hungover, huh? Well, stick out your hand. I've brought a lifesaver."

Blindly reaching out, hope sprang up as a warm cup touched her hands, spreading its warmth at the knowledge about what must be inside.

"Back up a step so I can close the door. It's so sunny, it would probably kill you if you opened your eyes."

Ari backed up two steps, then brought the cup to her mouth and sipped. "Mmm," she moaned as the chocolate and espresso passed her lips. "How did you know I would need this?"

Snickering, Denise grabbed her elbow, leading her to her favorite chair. "A little fairy told me. Now sit and rehumanize."

Sitting back, Ari sipped at the wonderful concoction, aware when the banging let up a little in her head. Cautiously, she blinked her eyes. The room was dark which helped tremendously. Looking around, her eyes fell on a blurry version of her friend, sitting across from her holding a bottle.

"A bit early to be drinking, isn't it?"

Chuckling, Denise put the bottle down. "Considering this was sitting by your computer, I assume you drink blogged last night?"

Frowning, Ari tried to remember. "I don't think so. I remember laughing a lot, though, so who knows?"

A small smile came to her lips as she remembered

her first few blogging attempts back in college. They were considered dull, boring, blasé, until she got drunk one night after a bad Jane-date. When she was drunk her filter did not exist, and what spewed out was as real as it could get. Her drink-blogging became a campus hit.

"Wait! I remember. I was filling out an online dating profile."

"And that made you laugh? I tried that once. Made me want to pull my hair out."

Chuckling as she started to feel human again, Ari nodded. "I got an agreement from Jane that if I joined three online dating sites and kept up with them she would stop dive-bomb dating me."

"Oh! Do you think she will actually keep to that agreement?"

"I hope so. She has such bad taste."

They chatted for an hour and by the time Denise left, Ari was able to open the blinds without wincing too badly.

After a long hot shower, she pulled on a pair of jeans and a sweater before turning on her computer. While it started up, she rifled through her fridge and freezer, trying to decide on lunch. She was so intent on her task that when her computer dinged to announce new emails, she jumped.

Laughing at her own nervousness, she closed the fridge, grabbed some crackers, and went back to the living room. Sitting on her desk chair, she put the crackers down and pulled up her email account. It took several seconds for the number of new emails to hit her.

"One hundred and fifty-seven? I've never received that many emails total in this account!" Sure, she was being spammed, she opened her inbox.

"Oh."

Only seven were spam messages, the rest were notifications from the three dating services. Some were notices that she was "liked." Whatever that meant. Others seemed to advertise guys she might like. Then, there were the messages from men.

Well, she hadn't gotten a master's degree in library science for nothing. Setting up new folders and rules, soon the emails were separated and catalogued. Now she could focus on what was important. Her eyes drifted to the trash making her snicker. "If I do that, Jane will find out and set me up with another loser.

"That reminds me."

Opening up a new message, she quickly sent an email off to her sister.

Jane,

Hope you are having a lovely Sunday. I am looking at 150 messages from three different dating sites. That should cover at least a couple months.

Just as a reminder, you still owe me the money for Jay.

See you Friday!

Ari

Snickering at the disgruntled expression that would most likely appear on her sister's face when she read it, she looked once again at the messages. Methodically, she went through each one, deleting the uninteresting ones, blocking the losers, and sighing at the tenth time she saw the same opening line. When she got to the last email and hit delete, she was exhausted. Looking at the clock, she could not believe she had just lost four hours.

"Well, that classifies as at least two dates," she grumbled, stretching and turning off the computer.

The rest of the day she found herself a bit restless. She went for a run in the park, and when she got home, she felt a pull toward her computer she had never felt before. Usually, she would turn it on maybe once a week, and then forget it was there.

"Must be all those emails. I don't ever want to go through that many at once again."

The next day was a free day. How she loved holidays. And she and Denise were going to the Reid Park Zoo. Denise was a supporter of the zoo, donating money to become a parent of one of the animals every year. On a monthly basis, she dragged Ari to ooh and ahh over her adopted pet. Ari hadn't minded when she supported the lion or the tiger. She even thought it was cool when Denise supported the lion-tail macaque. But this year, her friend supported the Visayan warty pig.

"A pig?" Ari moaned as Denise dragged her toward its pen. "Couldn't you have just gone and bought a ham?"

Denise let her go long enough to slap her arm. "Don't mention Dakila and ham in the same sentence! I don't want her to know I eat pork," she whispered, grabbing Ari again and pulling her forward.

As much as she teased Denise about it, Ari had to admit the pigs were rather cute. "I wish they had a male so we could see what they looked like." Males were reputed to have large manes that stuck up like a mohawk. She would love to see that.

After thirty minutes of oohing and ahing over Dakila, though Denise wasn't exactly positive which of the three was her pig so they raved over all three, they went to the gift shop and bought a few items for Ari's nieces and nephews. Ari wondered what the kids would think of the stuffed pigs.

After lunch at the Bamboo Club, Ari's favorite restaurant, Denise dropped her off at home. When she walked in the door, her eyes were drawn to her laptop and she chuckled. "Fine, obviously I must have some interest in this whole online dating thing as I can't stay away from the computer!"

After turning it on, she put away her leftovers and placed the bag of stuffed animals in a chest she kept for kiddie gifts. When Jane brought the little rugrats over, she hoped that would keep most of them busy. The problem was some of them were too old for stuffed animals. And the boys wouldn't be thrilled. "Oh well, maybe they can watch sports," she murmured, going over to sit down.

Pulling up her email, she watched as email after email went into its respective folder. Ninety-two new emails of which only one was spam. "This is crazy," she muttered even while recognizing there was something rather exciting about having so many men contact her, even if they weren't her type.

After going through each of the emails and deleting them all, she stared at the IDS folder she had created for the Interdimensional Dating Service. There was still only one email from them. Wondering why there was so much response from the others and not from them, she opened up their welcome email.

Miss Reynolds,

We thank you for joining the Interdimensional Dating Service. Only once before have we received an entry from your quadrant. As we want to make sure it was you who entered the profile information, please click on the link below and check the information. If you submitted and approve it, hit the approve button. It will become live within ten hours. If you did not, click the button that says delete. Your profile will be deleted immediately, and you will not be troubled by us again.

Interdimensional Dating Service

"Oh!" She hadn't gotten a response because they were waiting for her to approve the profile. Well, that made sense. Many websites did that nowadays. The way the note was written was still strange, but now the language seemed more formal, rather than having been written by someone who did not know English. And quadrant? She chuckled. They hadn't received anything from the southwest? How small was this site?

Clicking on the link, her screen flashed three times before settling on her profile. "Dang power," she sighed, knowing she was well overdue for a power outage.

Her profile surprised her. It was not anything like the others. On the other two sites a picture of her was plastered in the upper left corner and then all her information was displayed on the right in a question/answer type format. IDS obviously did things differently.

She had even been given her own URL and *menubar*. "That's shnazzy." The background looked almost like a picture of the mountains that could be seen from her living room window. Her photo looked as though it had been professionally altered. She looked really nice. They had even gotten rid of the small scar that marred her chin. And instead of a list of questions and answers, the profile had been separated into sections: Physical characteristics. Likes/Dislikes. Intelligence. Preferences. Cross-Dimensional Compatibility.

"I must have been tired when I started filling out the questions," she said as she looked it over. "Or it was the wine talking." None of her responses were written in question/answer format. Instead, each section was written out in a narrative, making her come alive. Whoever wrote her responses out in such a way had a wonderful, dry sense of humor, very much like her own.

After looking over the entire profile, she clicked the *Accept* button. Almost immediately, the urgency she felt about being on the computer seemed to leave. After turning it off, she went about her business. With only a four-day workweek ahead, plus the fact she needed to get caught up on all the lost hours from Friday, her life was about to get hectic.

Tuesday proved to be more than chaotic. From the moment she got into work at seven, she spent her time in front of her computer trying to enter the serials information she had not been able to complete the previous Friday. Unfortunately, while the network was just fine, she was not. To her utter annoyance, she kept typing the wrong items in, misspelling codes, and entering data into the wrong fields. Groaning, she turned off her monitor at lunch and went for a run. "Maybe a run will help my mind wake up."

When she left work a little after seven that evening, she just hoped the next day would be better. "A whole day of data entry down the tubes," she grumbled, wishing she could erase the entire day. Once she got home, she could not settle down, so instead of her normal Tuesday evening routine of dinner and reading, she changed into her workout clothes and went for another run.

It was already dark outside, but she made her way to the park and ran around it four times anyway, trying to wear herself out. It wore her body out, but her mind still churned madly away. Jogging up to her apartment, she was surprised to see a box sitting at the foot of the door. "I'm not expecting anything," she muttered, grabbing the box as she unlocked her door.

Once she got inside, she checked to make sure it was at the correct place. Yep, it was addressed to Miss Arwen Reynolds. "Definitely for me." Her eyes scanned the front of the small box, settling on the area where the return address would be. Instead of an address, some symbol was stamped there. She turned the box around several times, but could not make out what the symbol was.

Placing the box on the coffee table, she took off her jacket and shoes and went into the kitchen to make herself some hot chocolate. A box like this needed hot chocolate. As she poured the milk into the pan and pulled out the cocoa, her mind was on the box. What was in it? She wanted to go out and rip the box open, but she had never been spontaneous and was not about to do it now without her ritual.

Grinning, she thought back to how this ritual started. Her second year in college she received a box from an unmarked source, though she had known who it was from. Interest and yet worry about what could possibly be inside kept her from opening it immediately. Instead, she made herself a cup of strong hot chocolate with some Bailey's Irish Cream thrown in.

Once warm and buzzed, she had opened the package only to find some strange artifact from Asia, nothing else. The packages always came that way. Plain box, strange artifact of some sort, usually a statue and nothing else. No note, no letter, no invoice, no nothing. But then again, Abigail Bryory Reynolds, her ninety-one-year-old grandmother, did things like that. For her sixteenth birthday, Ari had been sent a phallic prayer deity.

Everything Abigail ever sent was tucked inside a chest in her closet, except for the deity statue. For some inexplicable reason, that sat on her night stand.

After mixing in the chocolate, she poured the wonderful mixture into a large mug, topping it off with the first alcohol her hands touched. Rum. Once the scent of heated rum reached her nostrils, she stopped pouring and placed the bottle back on the shelf. Then she took a sip.

"Yum! Everyone should drink hot chocolate like this."

Placing the mug in the living room next to the box, she went into her bedroom and changed into a pair of flannel pajama bottoms and a sweatshirt then went back into the living room. Taking the mug in one hand and the box in the other, she sat down on the sofa. Wanting to be buzzed enough for whatever Abigail sent her, she took several long pulls of her hot chocolate. "Mmmm," she sighed, placing it back on the coffee table.

"All right, Nana, here goes nothing." A small smile

passed over her lips as she imagined how Abigail's expression would look if she heard Ari call her Nana. Her little gray eyes would get tiny and turn dark.

"Look here, little girl," she would rasp in a voice broken from too much screeching, "I can still bend you over my knee and spank your bottom. I don't care if you are twenty-eight." As long as Ari could remember, her grandmother had insisted she be called Abigail. She even insisted that Ari's mother, her daughter Destra, call her by her given name.

Grabbing the letter opener from the coffee table, she cut through the tape, making sure not to push the metal too deep. Whatever was inside should not be marked up. One day, Abigail would return, and if anything she sent Ari was damaged…well, Ari did not want to know what would happen.

Jane and Cory were always interested to see what she got, because they didn't get anything interesting from their grandmother. Instead, they got books, electronics, dresses, hats, and any tourist stuff she thought they might like. Ari was the one she sent her odd, sometimes pornographic items to.

Placing the letter opener back onto the coffee table, she opened the box. It had been almost five years since she received anything from her grandmother. She could not wait any longer to see what she had been sent. Usually there would be tons of brown paper surrounding a brown paper wrapped package. Not in this box. To Ari's surprise there was a small wooden box that was almost the same size as the box it was in. On top of it was a piece of thick 8x10 paper folded in half. Abigail included a letter?

"She's never included a letter before." Picking up

the paper, she opened it up.

Miss Reynolds,

We are thrilled you have joined the Interdimensional Dating Service. Your profile is live and is already being searched by thousands of males across the dimensions. Over the next few days, you may experience some of the following symptoms.

Shortness of breath

Nausea

Tension

Cold shivers

Desire to return to your computer, again and again

We assure you these are natural responses to being a member of the Interdimensional Dating Service. They are the result of the interdimensional shift. We suggest alcohol as a suitable drink to help calm those responses.

As a thank you for being one of our female members, we have included a gift for you. Inside this box is an anklet made by the Faerce Jewelry Makers of Dimension Zeta. It was made specifically for you, and we promise it will bring you luck in your search.

If you have any questions, please contact us.

Interdimensional Dating Service

The giggle started out slow, but by the time she had read the note three times, Ari was laughing hard. "Oh, these people have a wonderful sense of humor! So this small gift is supposed to make me feel good about the hundred and forty-nine dollars I spent for three months membership?" Chuckling, she turned the outer box over and shook it until the box inside fell out.

Their dry sense of humor was wonderful! So many men did not understand when she made a joke. But if the men were anything like the writer of the note, she actually might find a guy she would enjoy dating.

As soon as the jewelry box hit her lap, she tossed the container over her shoulder and took hold of it. It was made from wood, but she could not tell what kind. It was smooth and had the most interesting veining ingrained in it. Turning it over, she gasped. The top was a piece of art in itself. The design looked familiar, but she could not place it right away.

Looking over to her cup of chocolate, she wanted a drink; but at the same time, she wanted to see what was inside the box more. Pulling the top off, she was impressed at how well the box was made. It fit tongue-in-groove perfectly with the bottom so that when they were together, you could barely see that it was not just one piece.

She was admiring the workmanship of the box when her gaze fell to the piece of jewelry sitting in the center. A small gasp escaped her lips as she studied it. It was thin and even in the dull light of her living room shone brightly. It wasn't gold or copper and, right off the top of her head, she could not place what type of metal it was. The only description that came to mind was "striking."

The anklet lay on a bed of what looked similar to velvet and stretched the width of the box. It was made of extremely thin pieces of the goldish metal interwoven to create a web of unmistakable beauty.

Unable to stop herself, she lifted it up out of the box. It felt weightless. "Wow," she whispered as she let it glide along her hands. She tried to bend it to see if she could, but each time she tried, the metal did not move. And yet when she laid it across her hand, it seemed to almost mold itself to her.

"Strange."

She jumped when her ringer went off. Laughing at her jumpiness, she put the anklet back in the box and reached for her phone. Almost immediately, she wanted to pick the piece of jewelry back up again.

"Hello?"

"Arwen Reynolds?" The voice on the line went in and out. Whoever it was must be in a bad cell area.

"Yes," she said slowly. "Who is this?"

"Stop whatever it is you are doing! You just do—" The line went dead.

Groaning, she checked caller ID. Out of area. "Well that helps," she groused.

The voice hadn't sounded familiar at all. In fact, she could not tell if it was a male or a female voice with how bad the reception was.

"Well. It is a Friday night. The teenagers must be bored." Placing her phone back down, she walked into her bedroom, at the moment forgetting all about the anklet.

As she stripped down, her sore muscles from all the running she had done that day returned. "I could use a bath." Walking into the bathroom, she was thrilled to turn on the one thing that sold her on the apartment in the first place—the large Jacuzzi tub. Turning the water on as hot as it would go, she plugged up the tub and walked away. It would take almost a half hour to fill.

After all her clothes were in the laundry basket, she went back out to finish her hot chocolate. As she grabbed the cup, her eyes once again fell on the jewelry box. Gulping the rest of her drink, she picked up the box with one hand and went into the kitchen. Placing the box down long enough to wash the cup seemed the most monumental of tasks, and she was not sure why.

"Must be because I have never seen anything this beautiful before."

Placing the cup on the drying rack, she took the box into her bedroom and went in to take her bath. Steam rose off the water and with a smile, she splashed a large amount of lavender oil into it before stepping in. A small hiss escaped her throat as she sank in, but she was not about to cool it down. "Feels wonderful," she sighed.

After the water filled completely, she turned it off and leaned back against the side, partially drifting in and out of sleep with the warmth and the fragrant scent of lavender that permeated the whole room and probably her entire apartment. There were two things keeping her from completely falling asleep though. The first was that odd phone call, the second was the anklet, which she was determined to try on once her bath was complete.

The phone call she would forget in time, so she tried to put it out of her mind. Must have been a wrong number, except they asked for her by name. Then it was a crank call.

When she tried not to think about the call, the anklet would come to mind. It was the most beautiful thing she had ever seen. All of the jewelry she owned was cheaply made, just costume jewelry that lasted a few months and then was thrown out or put aside for something new. But this piece...she could not imagine ever throwing it out. The makers of the anklet were listed on the note. She would have to look them up once she got out of the bath.

Usually one of her relaxation baths would take about an hour. This time she lasted twenty minutes, and that was only by sheer willpower. After getting out and drying off, she walked back into her bedroom where the beautiful box sat on top of her bed.

"There you are," she whispered, pulling the anklet out. It shimmered, even in the soft light of her bedroom. "Wow." Pulling her ankle up, she laid the anklet over it, excited about how nice it looked. She had always thought her ankles were shapeless, unattractive, but with this on, even they looked good. When she went to put it back inside the box, because after all it would be too scratchy to sleep in and she could wear it tomorrow, she found herself hooking the little clasp instead.

"Well, that is strange." Before she had hooked it, there had been room enough for her to place two fingers between it and her skin. Now, it fit her ankle like a glove. "So pretty." Standing up, she walked over to her full-length mirror and looked at it. "It looks like it is a part of my ankle."

The metal indeed looked as though it was embedded in the skin. "How odd." And yet, she could not find it within herself to remove it. "I will wear it until I go to bed and then remove it."

Grabbing one of her many books off a shelf, she settled onto her bed for a good read.

Blinking her eyes open, she stared around in surprise. "Wow, I must have fallen asleep." Stretching, she glanced over at her clock. "Four AM?" Well, she might as well get up. If she went back to bed now, she would be tired all day long.

The next few days were more than hectic. She worked from seven in the morning until after seven in the evening each day, trying to get caught up entering her serials information only to have the network go down every time she tried. The power definitely had it in for her. She would start typing, the computer screen would flash three times and then the network would go down. Frustrated, she spent much of her time checking messages on her phone and reading. Every evening she spent deleting stupidity emails. So far, she had not received any other ones from the Interdimensional Dating Service, but she was too busy to really think about it. So busy in fact, it never occurred to her that she hadn't removed her anklet once.

Until Friday night.

"So," Jane said brightly as she, Ari, and Cory sat down at their favorite Mexican restaurant to eat. "How is the online dating thing going?

Laughing, Cory turned to their waiter who appeared rather quickly. "Three jumbo margaritas. We're gonna need 'em."

While they waited for their drinks, Cory chatted about her newest client, and how he would not be pleased no matter how many times she changed his design. For someone who did not talk much as a rule, she never stopped except to take a breath. Once the drinks arrived, she sighed and leaned back. Glancing at Ari, she grinned. "All yours."

"Thanks." Ari shook her head in amusement. Leave it to Cory to find a way to stop the grilling until she could get some alcohol in her.

"So?" Jane encouraged, her eyes dancing.

"I got over a hundred emails on Sunday and ninety on Monday and since then ten to twenty per day." That seemed like a tremendous amount to Ari, and she felt it should meet if not exceed her quota.

"Yes, but did you respond to any of them?" Her sister was so eager for her response she leaned across the table.

Groaning, Ari took a large gulp of her drink. "No, none of them were...um..." She couldn't say "smart enough" because Jane would jump all over it. Before she could think of a thing to say, Jane jumped in anyway.

"Ari, it was just an opening email. Did you at least visit their profile?"

"No."

Sighing in exasperation, Jane turned away for a couple minutes. The other two could hear her counting under her breath, something their mother used to do before she would explode.

"Gotten responses from all three?" Cory asked to try and push back the inevitable Jane eruption.

"No, actually. Plenty of responses from OKdate and Matchinone.com, but nothing from the dimensional one."

Jane's head swung around. "Did you fill out their questionnaires? They have all sorts of psychology tests that help to match you with the right one."

Ari wasn't about to admit she filled the profile out when drunk. She was sure that would elicit a bad response. Besides, the profile ended up looking amazing anyway. "Yeah, I filled out everything I could find. The profile looks great. They even made my picture look fantastic."

When the waiter came to take their orders, Ari took a deep breath and tried to figure a way out of this conversation. It was not going well. As soon as the waiter left, Jane turned on her again.

"Well, you need to take the upper hand, Arwen. Go surf some profiles, contact these men. If the right ones aren't contacting you, go find them."

The feeling of being cornered overcame her and without realizing she was doing it, she reached down and stroked her anklet underneath her pants' leg.

Oh, please something stop Jane.

The lights flickered on and off three times, and then to Ari and Cory's surprise, Jane changed the subject and did not bring it up the rest of dinner.

As she headed home, Ari groaned at how stiff she was. "I guess I was a bit stressed." She had assumed at some point, Jane would bring up dating again, but she hadn't, which was really strange and very un-Jane like. After parking her car, she got out and headed toward her front door, glad the weekend had arrived.

Chapter Four - *First Contact*

After turning on her computer the moment she walked in the door, Ari set about fixing herself a drink. Of course she had three margaritas during dinner, so she really should not push it, but it was a Friday night, so what would it matter?

Heading back to her computer, she brought up her email account. "Seventy-five?" she snorted, placing her drink down. "Guys must use the weekends to…" It occurred to her they must be bored and home on a Friday night as well. "How sad. We are all in the same boat."

She sipped her drink as the incoming mail separated itself into the folders, her eyes flashing to the IDS folder every few seconds. So far, no new emails. Shrugging, but not really understanding why she was not garnering the interest from there as she had from the other two sites, she started opening up emails. When she deleted all of them, she went to delete trash, surprised to find only seventy-two emails there. Looking back at her folders, her heart went bu-bump rather loudly. There were three emails in the IDS folder.

As she moved the mouse toward that folder, she was surprised to find her hand shaking. "Well, that is weird." But then again, maybe not. She was more excited about emails from this particular dating service for some reason. It just seemed more like her. Closing her eyes for a moment, she took a deep breath. Then, after opening them, she clicked on the folder.

Her eyes flitted over the subject lines.

You have mail from CunninglyStupid
You have mail from AttractivelyAgile
You have mail from DerangedLegophile

Snickering at the user names, she opened the first one. She had to see what CunninglyStupid had to say.

> *Well, I must say, your profile was quite refreshing. So unlike what most females post online. We seem to have many of the same interests. I, also, enjoy reading, running, and trying out new food.*
>
> *Do you enjoy Corofus?*

She blinked. Corofus? What is Corofus? Before checking out his profile, she went on to the message by AttractivelyAgile.

> *BeautifullyCorruptible,*
>
> *What a lovely username. One I would love to hear more about. I am a relatively attractive man in the prime of his life looking for a partner for laughter, fun, and travel as well as lots and lots of sex.*
>
> *Interested? I am unfamiliar with your quadrant. Can you jump dimensions easily?*

Snorting, she took a gulp of her drink. Well, you couldn't say he wasn't blunt about his interests. And another comment about her quadrant. What did people think about the southwest anyway? It wasn't like she was in some unknown country. She glanced once again at the name he had called her. Why would he call her that? Her username was Arwen1984.

Sighing, she went on to the last one, DerangedLegophile. Did that mean he loved legos?

It is a pleasure to meet you, beautiful lady. Your profile is magnificent. Would you like to meet? I have a pass-through for the shift if you would like to do dinner.

Shaking her head, she went back to the first message. Three different messages, all of them somewhat confusing. Clicking on the link that would show her CunninglyStupid's profile, she jumped when the screen flashed three times, went black, and then went to a blank webpage. Confused, she closed down her browser and went back and clicked the link again. It did the same thing, except this time instead of a blank webpage, it said "your information is currently downloading".

Looking at the percentage downloading, she grimaced as it said '1% downloading'. "His profile must be more intense than mine." Minimizing that window, she went back to her emails and clicked the links for the other two guys. With each one, her screen flashed several times and a blank screen came up that switched to a download screen a few seconds later.

"This is going to take forever," she moaned. Turning off her monitor, she grabbed her drink and went to change her clothes.

Once changed into her pajamas along with booties to keep her feet warm, she went back into the living room. Turning on her monitor, she looked at the percentages. All three were about twenty-five percent. Shrugging, she left the monitor on and curled up in her favorite chair while turning on her television. Absentmindedly, she rubbed her fingers over her anklet, which calmed her almost immediately. To her surprise her computer chimed and when she looked over at it, a profile page was sitting on her screen.

"Oh!" Well that was faster than she expected. Jumping up, she put her drink down and plopped down at her desk. The profile was for CunninglyStupid. He looked tall, thin, and rugged, with dark curly hair, a heavy mustache, and what looked to be a hint of danger surrounding him.

"Like I can tell that from a photo," she laughed softly. He was wearing pants and a sleeveless top, which showed off a rather large tattoo on his shoulder, but she had no idea what it was of. One thing that surprised her was how his profile was laid out so differently than her own. While hers had been separated into sections, his was one narrative of his life. Without thinking about it, she began to read.

Greetings from Gordron!

Here in the high dimension, we are suffering from a long drought...of females. For thousands of years, we have had to grieve through this humiliation, but all hope is not lost. You are reading my profile! This gives me hope, dear lady.

For a brief history of myself. I was engaged in both the Corolean War and the Inter-Dimensional Conflict. In the latter, I was in charge of the legion that took down the Brinian invasion. Nobody has ever bested me in a fight. I can and will protect you.

What would you achieve by becoming the mate of a Gordron warrior? Why, my lady, anything your heart desired. You would have

the finest jewelry and lace at your fingertips,
the best food and slaves for your comfort. You
would want for nothing.

All that awaits, is for you to reach out to
me. I await your note, my dear sweet lady.
Contact me soon.

Ari wasn't sure whether to laugh or roll her eyes. It was obvious this guy must be into one of those role-playing games. A Gordron warrior? Giggling drunkenly, she closed down his profile and deleted his email. Definitely not for her, though he did give her a good laugh.

Pulling up the profile for AttractivelyAgile, she was surprised and a bit unnerved by his photo. Instead of a full face-shot like hers, or a full body shot like CunninglyStupid, his face was in shadow. It looked as though the picture had been taken from above. The only thing she could clearly see were his eyes, which blazed red. Gasping she sat back in her chair. "Well, he wants to scare some people!"

At first, she just wanted to shut down the window and forget him, but she decided to read his profile anyway. It was set up into two sections, one about him and one about what he was looking for. Taking a deep breath, she began to read about him.

I am pure power, can you handle me? You
will kneel at my feet and do as I say, purely at
my side for my amusement and enjoyment...

She shut down the window and deleted his email. "Idiot."

All that was left was the third profile. Groaning, as she wasn't sure she wanted to see it, she opened up the window anyway. "Oh dear." Her lips twitched with amusement. The image was of a very large Lego. "Well, at least he has a sense of humor."

There wasn't much to his profile. She wasn't sure if he was hiding something, or if he did not have much to say.

I am a Quartermaster of the Keylon Realm. We live quiet peaceful lives and while I wish to live out the rest of my days here, I am willing to travel anywhere to meet the next lady of my dreams. Are you her? I will cross any dimension, climb any tower, defeat any beast to win your heart. If you are to fit in with my forty-two wives, you must...

Squealing with laughter, Ari bent over, grasping her stomach. "So he is a role-player with tons of wives? No, thank you." Snorting with laughter, she closed his profile and deleted his email. "Well, one thing I will say about IDS. Their men at least give me a laugh."

After closing the computer down, she realized she was feeling a little nauseated. "Too much alcohol." Groaning, she washed her cup and went to bed. Curling up in the warmth of her bed, she fell asleep, her hand stroking her anklet.

The next day she spent out of her apartment, running at the park, going to lunch with Denise, having afternoon coffee with her friends Luis and Trevor. She figured getting those three emails from IDS quelled her desire for online dating sites since she had not had an inkling to check her computer so far for the day. That changed at exactly 5:02. She was wearing a long denim skirt and had just crossed her left leg over her right, thus showing her ankles for the first time that day.

"Ari!" Trevor exclaimed, looking at her foot.

"Where did you get that?"

Looking down, she blushed slightly looking at the anklet. Each time she looked at it, she loved it more and more. It felt as though it was becoming an integral part of her. "Oh, just a gift from a friend." She passed it off with a smile.

He looked into her eyes and a slow grin spread across his face. "Well, well, well, looks like Ari has found herself a man, a man with money."

Luis looked around him and focused on the piece of jewelry. A low whistle left his lips. "Holy shit, Ari. What did you do for that?"

Frustrated and a little embarrassed about how she had come to own the beautiful item, she glared at him. "Nothing! Well, nothing bad anyway. I joined an online dating site and this was one of their gifts for joining."

He let out another low whistle and winked at her while leaning back against his life partner. "Well, if that is the kind of stuff they are giving out…if Trevor and I ever break up, I want the URL."

"Excuse me." The three of them turned to look at the barista who was standing at their table looking amused.

"Yes?"

The girl handed Ari a large drink. "It is a large white chocolate latte from the tall man in the gorgeous suit over by the door. He said to give it to the girl with the fancy anklet." Following the direction the girl was pointing, Ari caught sight of a tall, thin man in what looked to be a very expensive suit. She could not see what he looked like because he wore a large hat that threw a shadow on three-quarters of his face, but there was no doubt as she looked at him, two things

47

happened at the same time.

First, he raised his fingers to his hat, tapped the rim, and then walked out. Second, she let out a little squeak as her left ankle burned slightly.

The other three laughed and the barista walked away fanning herself. "Well, looks like you caught some rich guy's attention," Trevor said with a wicked grin. "Maybe that piece of jewelry is a talisman to draw rich men to you."

"Yes," Luis chimed in, grinning. "Or at least a good luck charm."

Rolling her eyes, Ari rubbed at her ankle where the burn had stopped. She put up with their ribbing for another thirty minutes before they all needed to go. When she left, she dropped the untouched coffee in the trash. She had been too uncomfortable to drink it in front of the guys and now it was cold anyway.

As she got into her car the desire to check her computer came on her quickly, so quickly in fact she was out of the parking lot and two-thirds the way home before she even realized it. By the time she pulled into the parking lot, she felt anxious for some reason, as though if she did not check her computer, something bad would happen.

Reminding herself that, that was a stupid thought, she nevertheless jogged the short distance from her car, quickly letting herself inside and turning on the computer. For once, she did not go and do other things while it booted up. Instead, she sat while impatiently tapping her foot as the clunker went through its paces. "Hurry up," she hissed, starting to drum her fingers on the desk.

As the windows screen came up and she poised her

hand over the mouse, her phone started to ring. "No!" she exclaimed, unsure as to why she was being so jumpy. Pulling the phone out of her pocket, she checked the caller id. Out of area. Groaning, she accepted the call.

"Yes?" she snapped.

"Arwen?" She immediately recognized the voice as the one from days ago.

"Who is this?"

"Arwen! I've been trying to get hold of you for days, honey! It's Abigail."

Abigail? Her mouth dropped open. What was her grandmother calling her for? She never called. "Abigail?" she said cautiously.

"Yes!" her grandmother said, her line cutting in and out, filled with static. "Look, I don't have much time, but have you done anything strange lately?"

Ari snorted. "Strange? Not that I know of." Her life was a veritable pile of boredom interspersed with the occasional blasé moment.

A loud sigh drifted through the phone. "Are you sure?"

"Abigail? What could I have done? I work twelve hours a day during the week, go out with friends on the weekend. I don't have time to do anything strange." Except for some online dating, but nowadays that was not so strange.

"Hmm, well then, I don't know what the psychic was talking about."

"Psychic?" Ari barely held back a snort.

"Yes, I saw a psychic a few days ago. She told me my granddaughter was getting into something she would not be able to handle. I tried calling you that night, but my phone cut off. Seems," she chuckled, "that I have been all upset over nothing. So, I have a minute or two left, how is my favorite grandchild doing?"

"I won't tell Jane and Cory you said that," Ari said dryly, making her grandmother laugh.

"Oh, Cory is all right, but Jane needs to stop being so stuffy. Tell me, are you enjoying your life, Arwen?"

Gnawing on her lip for a moment, Ari was surprised to find herself rubbing her anklet. Almost immediately, her eyes were drawn to her email screen where there were one hundred and five new emails. "My life is okay. Nothing to complain about." Even as the words passed her lips, she knew how untrue they were, but would not take them back for anything.

"Uh-huh," Abigail said, sounding unconvinced. "Well, I need to go, honey. There is not a lot of cell service where I am. Just promise you will think carefully about anything fun or exciting before you do it, okay?"

"Sure, Nana," she sighed, snickering when she heard Abigail's intake of breath.

"Arwen Reynolds, I to—" The line cut off.

Grinning, she pocketed the phone. It had been nice actually to hear from her grandmother for once. She would have to send a message to Cory and Jane telling them Abigail was seeing a psychic now. That should give them a good chuckle.

Turning back to her computer screen, she looked at the folders. Most of the messages were from the boring sites, but there were four from IDS. Ignoring all the other emails, she opened up the IDS folder, scratching her ankle when it tingled. Her eyes ghosted over each note's subject.

You have mail from CourageousKaro
You have mail from TemperedAlbino
You have mail from CalliperedStresser
You have new mail from AttractivelyAgile

Surprised she had a second email from the weirdo with red eyes who wanted a woman to kneel at his feet, she concentrated on the first three. All three were similar and before going on to AttractivelyAgile's message, she visited their profiles.

CourageousKaro's picture reminded Ari of what she always thought a gnome would look like, long curly white beard and bushy eyebrows included. Once again, she saw a narrative only and wondered if most men's profiles were like that.

I am from Beysa Minor. For the last decade I have been involved with the Dolotheon Conflict...

Groaning, she went to the next. What was it with men and war? Did they honestly expect to get a girl with such talk? Besides, she was beginning to think the guys who subscribed to the site were either mentally unbalanced or teenagers who spent their days role-playing. She quickly skimmed through the other two profiles before closing them and going back to email. "Okay, Agile, let's see what you have to say today."

My dear Corruptible,

I apologize, I could not wait. After seeing your beautiful face, I could just imagine it in the most delicious of expressions. Pain, pleasure, fear, desire, hate, love. It is all there and I can hardly wait to see it in person. Write back to me so we can make this connection.

Orion

P.S. Do you truly enjoy chocolate in your coffee?

A chill went up her spine at the same time a sharp burn spread across her ankle. "Ouch!" she hissed, reaching down to rub it. This character sounded dangerous. Who would want to see pain, fear, and hate in someone's expression? "Sicko," she grumbled, clicking on his profile link. There had to be a way to block him and now seemed the time.

As she waited through the strange flashes and then as his profile downloaded, his postscript flitted through her brain. *Do you truly enjoy chocolate in your coffee?* A flash of the strange man standing by the door, his face in shadow came into her mind. "No, no way! There is no way he could know who I was, let alone where I would be. No."

And yet, the constant burning of her ankle and the queasiness in her stomach told her something was wrong here. Why would he have mentioned chocolate and coffee if he did not send it to her at the coffee shop? And yet the possibility he could be the man in the coffee shop had to be astronomical, didn't it?

His profile popped up, and she tried to ignore his picture and narrative while she looked around for a block button. The nausea in her stomach and burn in her ankle increased the longer she stayed on the page, but she could not find what she needed. "Fine!" she finally called aloud as she closed the screen, giving a small whimper of relief when her ankle stopped burning.

Quickly deleting the email from the scary man, she was startled to see a new message in the box.

You have mail from CuriosityLemmings

She stared at the email suspiciously. So far, the emails from IDS had not been normal in any way, and the profiles were even worse. Did she even want to open this one? A small tingle in her ankle seemed to make the nausea go away, and before she even realized she was doing it, she opened the message.

Why is it first messages are so difficult to write? I mean, it should be very easy to write something like "I am fantastically wonderful and your soulmate," but not only is that not easy, it would be a lie as that is not something we can tell, now is it?

My name is Terrian, and I live in a library. I know, exciting right? Well, actually it is not. I live in the largest library in our largest city. We serve over a million residents of our fine hamlet. It is my job to make sure everything is up to date, so our fair citizens have access to all the newest information out there. I spend most of my day around books and technology devices, so unfortunately I do not get the time to date much.

Which is why I joined the Interdimensional Dating Service. My brother met his mate here, and I figured I would give it a try. No harm in trying, right?

You sound like a very interesting woman from your profile, not to mention, absolutely stunning, and I would love to learn more about you. You mention you love books. What are your favorites? From your neck of the woods, I prefer Aristotle and Shakespeare. They make me think, laugh, and think some more.

Well, that is all I will say for now. I hope to hear back.

Terrian

"Wow, he actually sounds human," she snickered. "What's he doing on this website?" A feeling she could not describe started at her ankle and moved its way up her leg. It wasn't unpleasant, though she did not think she could classify it as pleasant either. It just was.

Figuring she might as well check out his profile so she could cross him and IDS off her list permanently, she clicked the link. To her surprise, it downloaded much faster than the others had, right after her screen flashed three times. She stared at the image on the screen for several minutes without moving. Her mind was having a hard time making sense of what she saw. Terrian looked...normal, in a strange sort of way.

In the black and white photo, he had dark hair that came to his shoulders, dark eyes, and very angular features. His eyes looked directly into the camera and something about them made her heart skip a few beats and then take off as though it was in a race. He was sexy, there was no doubt, and yet compared to the others, he felt normal to her, even though something in the back of her head kept saying there was something off about his photo. Maybe it was the nice message he wrote that made him feel so normal.

When she was finally able to tear her gaze away from his picture, she looked at his narrative, hoping against hope he wasn't going to talk about war.

Everyone has something to say on these things, but most of what could be said should be saved for a face-to-face meeting. So, I will give you an overview. I live a rather lonely life. My work and position make it so I cannot get out and just date, as much as I would prefer to be doing so. I come from a very large family and am the only unmated sibling left, much to my parents' disapproval and my brothers' amusement.

For everyone there comes a time in their life where they are just ready to meet that special someone. I suppose I have finally reached that time. Ask yourself the following questions. If your answers are yes, I look forward to getting to know you.

Terrian

Q1. Can you handle stress well?

Q2. Do you enjoy silence?

Q3. Do you feel as though magic surrounds us all, coming out at the strangest times to make us notice?

*Q4. Do you like me so far? *wink**

Laughing in delight at his friendly profile, Ari bounced softly in her seat. Finally, here was a possibility! He sounded nice and had a great sense of humor not to mention his picture was attractively normal. Sitting up straight, she minimized the profile and went back to his message, clicking the link to reply.

Terrian,

Thanks so much for your message. Yours is the first one I have received that did not make me shudder. I have no issues with you living in a library as so do I. I prefer to spend my time around books. They are non-judgmental...well most of the time. Ha ha.

Aristotle and Shakespeare. Interesting duo. Can you imagine those two standing toe-to-toe having a discussion? Something tells me Aristotle would get annoyed first, if he did not try to come on to Shakespeare that is.

Your life sounds as lonely as mine. I have a few friends I go out with on the weekends, and I see and talk to my two sisters on a weekly basis, but my mother left us a decade ago. I have never met my father and my only other living relative, my grandmother, traipses around the planet digging up things and sending them to me.

To be honest, I only joined this website because my sister Jane kept setting me up with the strangest men and we came to an agreement that if I joined an online dating service, she would stop. Up until your note and profile, I was sure the universe was filled with losers. Now, I might possibly change my mind.

I look forward to your next note,

Arwen

Taking a deep breath, she pushed the send button, hoping she didn't come across as, as much of an idiot as she usually did with men she was interested in.

For some reason, she felt exhausted, as though reading and writing the message had taken everything out of her. Shutting down her computer, she changed into pajamas and went to bed. Maybe an early night would help. The instant her head hit the pillow, she fell asleep, two pairs of eyes watching her in her dreams. One pair was dark, intelligent, caring. The other was intense, sinister, evil. No matter how hard she tried, she couldn't shake either of them. Four times, she awoke in a sweat calling out for a person she had never met.

"I must be going crazy," she murmured the fourth time she woke up. Her ankle tingled as if to agree, and she slipped once again into sleep.

Chapter Five - *The Shift Bracelet*

Tapping her fingers on her leg, Ari stared out her living room window at the mountains outside. She hadn't slept well the night before and was feeling jumpy. Added to that, she had agreed when Jane asked to come over with her three youngest children for brunch. Glancing over toward her computer, which she had studiously ignored all morning, her eyes caught sight of the three ugly stuffed pigs she got at the zoo. Hopefully, her nieces would like them.

Glancing at the clock ticking madly away on the wall, she was disgruntled to see only two minutes had passed since the fifteen or so since she last looked at it. Jane was not set to arrive for another thirteen minutes, and knowing her sister, it would be more likely to be thirty. Given she had thirty minutes, her eyes slid back over to her computer. Would Terrian have replied already?

"No," she quickly said, taking a deep breath. She was not going to be one of those girls who waited with baited breath, or other such nonsense, for some guy to contact her. Leaning over, it took a moment before she realized she was rubbing her ankle again.

Groaning, she leaned back. Ever since she had put the anklet on, she always seemed to be touching it. To her embarrassment, even though she would not admit it to anyone else, she had not removed it since she put it on. She tried once and had a tiny panic attack. So far, it hadn't tarnished at all, so she assumed getting the metal wet was not hurting it in any way.

Glancing up again at the clock, she grimaced. "Someone has slowed down time."

A knock on her door surprised her. For one thing, Jane was never early; for another, she would have expected to hear Jane's three children as they came up to her place. They were not exactly quiet. Walking quickly to her door, she opened it with a smile on her face, ready to greet her nieces, but there was no one there.

Surprised, she placed her hands on the door jamb and leaned forward looking both ways. Not a person was in sight. "Hello?" she called. No answer. As she pulled back to close the door, something caught her eye. Looking down, she was surprised to see a flower wrapped in tissue paper lying at her doorstep. At least she thought it was a flower. She had never seen anything quite like it.

Leaning forward, she picked it up, a loud cry leaving her lips as her ankle flared with pain. "Crap!" she hissed, hopping back on her good ankle while shutting the door. "What is with my ankle? Am I allergic to my anklet?"

That made her freeze. She did not want to be allergic to her jewelry because that would mean she would have to remove it. Hopping into her kitchen, she laid the flower down on the countertop and leaned over to get a vase, sighing in relief as the burn became less intense.

"Maybe it is time to remove it, at least for a few hours," she tried to convince herself as she poured water into the vase. "At least to check for a rash or something." Her fingers reached out for the flower and the second they made contact, her ankle once again burst into shards of stinging pain.

Screaming, she dropped the flower and grabbed hold of her ankle, hopping back and forth on her one foot as she tried desperately to unhook the anklet. "Crap, crap, crap," she hissed as tears ran down her cheeks. Hopping to the closest chair, she sat down and scrambled for the clasp on the anklet. It seemed to take forever as she fiddled around it, trying to find the small item. Finally, when she was about to pull out some ice and pour it over her foot, she found it.

Grasping the small lever, she pulled and screamed.

The lever pulled back, but when she pulled at the metal to pull it off her ankle, it seemed to be adhered to her skin. Yanking at it, she finally made it budge, letting out another scream when her skin tore. "Holy crap! What am I going to do? The thing has become a part of me!" Before she could try to think logically, noise erupted from her doorway.

"Auntie Ari!" three tiny voices called.

"Crap!" Ari looked at her ankle where a thin line of blood visibly trickled down her foot and between her toes. Grabbing the closest hand towel, she shut the lever on the clasp to keep it in place until she could have it removed and wrapped the towel over it.

"Just a minute!" she called back, standing up and limping slightly out to the living room.

Jane was getting the girls settled on the couch so at first she did not notice her sister. When she did look over, her eyes narrowed. "Ari, what's wrong?"

Shaking her head and putting on a fake smile, Ari

smiled at her nieces. "Hey, Kari, Nell, Shasta, guess what I have for you?"

"What Auntie Ari?" they chimed together, making her grin. Who knew identical triplets could be so cute? They all had their father's coloring with their bright red hair and deep green eyes. Add in their cherubic faces, and she didn't see how anyone could not fall in love with them on sight.

Grabbing the pigs, she tossed them at the girls. With squeals of delight, they wrestled with them, and before long they were playing quite happily, ignoring the two adults in the room.

"While they are playing, let's take care of that foot," Jane said quietly, grabbing Ari's hand and dragging her into the kitchen. While Ari watched her, Jane efficiently put the flower in the vase and placed it on the counter before wetting down a couple of hand towels. Then she walked past Ari, returning a few minutes later with antibiotic cream and some bandages.

"So, what happened?" she asked, patting the countertop as her way of giving Ari the direction to hop up there.

"Not sure." Ari winced, hopping over and up onto the fake granite. "I got this anklet about a week ago and it has been just fine, but for the last day I've been having some reactions to it. When I tried to remove it, I tore my skin."

Shaking her head, Jane removed the towel and quickly cleaned up the dried blood. Turning Ari's ankle this way and that, she asked, "How does it feel now?"

"It is still burning."

Frowning, Jane looked up at her. "Where's the clasp?"

"Oh, it's hard to find. Just a second." Fumbling around, Ari found the small lever. "Here." She pulled it up gingerly and left it.

Jane grabbed the lever and lifted it slightly. "Oh dear, I see what you mean." Letting her fingers trail along the top of the anklet, she tried to get her nails underneath it. "Um, Ari? The whole thing seems stuck to your ankle. What's it made of?"

"I'm not quite sure."

Turning, Jane exited the kitchen for a moment, coming back with some hydrogen peroxide. "Place your ankle over the sink."

Knowing she looked real stupid, Ari moved as quickly as possible to do so. Her ankle still burned and she wanted the thing off...almost as much as she wanted to leave it on. Jane poured the peroxide on top of the jewelry making Ari squeak.

"Oh, don't be a baby," Jane chided.

"It's not that," Ari whined. "Don't hurt the anklet."

Jane looked up at her, her mouth partially open. "Don't hurt the anklet? Ari, this thing is hurting you."

"I don't care. I will wear something between the anklet and me if I have to, but I don't want to lose it."

Rolling her eyes, once again Jane tried to run her fingernail between the anklet and Ari's skin. "Shit!" Jane hissed.

"What?" Ari cried out, afraid Jane had broken it.

Lifting her hand, Jane showed off her extremely nice manicured set of nails. Except for one which was now torn.

"Oh." Ari looked at her sister in surprise. Jane had had long fingernails as long as Ari had remembered; ever since their mother had allowed her to get her first manicure. "What happened?"

"The anklet just severed the nail. How strange." Not to be deterred, Jane grabbed the peroxide, lifted up the latch, and poured it where the skin had torn.

A hiss escaped Ari's lips, but that was all the sound she made as the cold liquid met her torn skin.

"Well, there are no bubbles, so at least there is no infection," Jane said cautiously, as she pulled lightly at the anklet, trying to make it come away from her sister's body. Finally, she re-latched the clasp and looked up. "Ari, I think you need to go to the emergency room and have that thing removed."

Groaning, Ari shook her head. She hated doctors and hospitals more than anything in the world. Even if she didn't, she had the feeling they would be more likely to want to cut it off and she was not about to allow that. "I'm sure it will come off. Later, I will take a nice hot bath, and I bet it releases then."

Frowning, Jane rinsed Ari's ankle and wrapped it in gauze. "Well, keep an eye on it. If it looks like it is becoming infected, call me, and I will take you to the emergency room right away." She stood up and leveled her most motherly gaze at Arwen. "Tomorrow you call your normal doctor and have him remove it. Understand?"

Groaning, Ari whipped her body around and hopped off the counter, only wincing slightly as she landed. "Yes, Mom."

Smiling, Jane turned to the flower. "Where did you get this? It's quite beautiful."

Ari's eyes settled on the strange flower that had three deep red petals shaped like helicopter blades surrounded by a bevy of white fuzz. The center of the flower was a deep black, deeper than she had seen in any flower before. It was captivating and rather unsettling to look at.

Shaking her head, Ari took the vase, hissing as the burn exploded in her ankle, but tried to ignore it, at least as long as Jane was nearby. "Somebody left it on my doorstep. I'm not even sure what kind of flower it is."

"It's gorgeous. When you find out, let me know. I would love to have some in the house."

After placing the flower on her bedside table, she went back into the living room, glad the burn was settling into just heat. Now it felt like a light sunburn—that she could handle.

For two hours, Ari and her sister talked and played with the triplets while eating the cinnamon rolls Jane brought. It was so nice Ari practically forgot how bossy Jane had been about men lately. Almost as soon as she thought that, Jane ruined it.

"So, any interesting men online?" Jane asked without looking at her sister.

Shaking her head at the irony, she wondered if she hadn't thought it would Jane have mentioned anything, Ari nodded. "Well, most of the emails have been from dorks, but I did get a really nice message last night from a guy that sounds…decent."

Jane whipped her head around so fast, Ari was surprised her sister didn't get whiplash. Jane beamed. "Oh, do tell."

Grinning, Ari told her the little she knew. "Well, I've just received the one email and sent one back, but he seems nice. He works in a library, too. Terrian also seems to have a great sense of humor."

"Terrian?" Jane asked with interest. "Oooh, that's the kind of name for tall, dark, and handsome heroes in romance novels. Is he tall, dark, and handsome?"

Laughing, Ari shrugged. "Well, he seems to be dark and handsome. I don't know how tall he is. Did I mention, he has a great sense of humor?"

"Ooh!" she said, her eyes bright and wide. "Which site was it from?"

"The dimension one."

"Uh-huh, uh-huh," Jane responded eagerly. "Erica and Danielle both met their husbands through there and said they knew there was something special about the guy with the first message." Squealing she jumped up and hugged Ari, embarrassing her little sister. "Oh, I know you are going to meet someone wonderful, Arwen." Clapping her hands just like her daughters, she turned her attention back to them.

By the time they left thirty minutes later, Ari felt really good about Terrian's message and decided to check for a new one. The burn in her ankle was negligible now, so she turned on the computer and sat back. Once her email program was up and running, she waited impatiently for the messages to find their folders. Out of thirty new messages, two dropped into the IDS folder. Deleting all the others without even looking at them, she opened up IDS.

Immediately disappointment and annoyance hit her. Neither message was from CuriousityLemmings, but one was from AttractivelyAgile. "This guy just won't give up!" Shaking her head, she deleted his message without looking at it. The other message was from some guy called DaringlyGauche. Upset, she closed down the computer. She would look at his message and profile later. Looking at it right now, he really did not stand a chance. She was frustrated at herself for being disappointed because Terrian had not written back yet and bothered that Agile, or Orion as he had called himself, had.

Leaning back, she looked down at her ankle, frowning as all she could see was the gauze her sister had wrapped around it. "Oh please be an easy fix," she sighed. "I don't want to have to lose you."

The rest of the day, she did not feel like doing much. Putting any weight on her left foot made it achy, plus she felt continuously nauseated. After downing some leftovers, she decided a nap was in order. Closing her blackout curtains, she settled into her bed, wincing as the burn came back slightly. Even with the pain, her eyes began to close the second her head hit the pillow. The last thing she saw before she fell asleep was the strange little flower that seemed to be watching her.

Blinking her eyes open, Ari stared around her. Where was she? She knew she had pulled her blackout curtains, but her room had never been this dark before. Also, it was cold, so cold she felt it clear through to her bones. Shivering, she reached out for her covers, but found none. "What the—" Her exclamation was cut off as her hand went to lean on her bed but instead touched something cold and hard. Stone.

Sitting up, she started to feel around her. She wasn't on her bed, but was lying on a cold, hard floor. As she got used to the darkness, she expected to see something, but so far everything was pitch black. "Hello?" she called out, afraid, and yet feeling stupid for being afraid. This could not be real, could it?

At first there was no response, but then she heard a

c-clap, c-clap, c-clap sound that reminded her of boots walking along a cobblestone walkway. They became louder and she knew they were coming closer. Gulping, she gazed in the direction she thought they were coming from. "Ah," said a smooth cold voice, "my pet has awakened." A loud squeak jarred her mind, making her body shudder. It sounded like an old iron gate that needed oiling.

The quick sound of a match being lit and the flicker of fire and candle coming together met her senses. The light wasn't much, as it was still quite a ways away from her, but it allowed her to see a man in dark pants and a dark shirt walking toward her, the candle in his hand. Her eyes darted to where his face would be, but it was in shadow.

Everything within her started to shiver as she stared at the man holding the candle as he came closer and closer. When he was a few feet away, he stopped. "Has my pet come to terms with her enslavement?" he purred softly.

She gulped. "Who-who are you?"

He chuckled. It was not a pleasant sound. "Ah, pet, I am your master. I have been since before I found you." He reached out a hand to touch her, and she shrunk back reflexively. "Do not move away!" he snapped, his voice colder than ice. Moving quicker than she expected, his hand grabbed her jaw, and he turned her face toward him. It must have been her nerves, but she could have sworn the instant he touched her, a strange thrum went through her body. His voice became a low rumbling purr again that made her relax. "Now, pet, again I ask, are you willing to accept your enslavement?"

For some reason unknown to her, she wanted to say yes, but a pain started in her ankle, and it was quickly gaining in intensity and moving up her leg. "Let me go!" she cried out in a whisper.

"Go where, pet? You are in my dungeon, on my estate. There is nowhere for you to go until I am finished with you, and I have no intention of finishing with you for years. " His words were still spoken in that slow, hypnotic purr, and unconsciously she leaned in toward him. The change in her position allowed her to see his face, and she quickly flashed to his eyes. Their bright red irises caused a terror that made the hair on her arms stand on end.

"NO!" she screamed as the pain in her ankle exploded.

Sitting straight up, Ari looked around her bedroom, breathing in short desperate gasps. "It was a dream, just a dream," she whimpered as she clutched her ankle, which was searing like crazy.

Reaching up to her face, she felt the tears leaking from her eyes. "That was the scariest dream I have ever had. Why would Orion appear in my nightmares?"

Pulling herself out of the mess she had made of the blankets, Ari stumbled her way into her bathroom, wincing at the pain in her leg. "Need to get this off," she whimpered as she started her bath. Quickly stripping, she slowly unwrapped the gauze from around her ankle and slipped into the bath before it was even a quarter-way filled. She still shivered from her nightmare and needed the warmth the bath could and would provide.

Leaning back, she tried to breathe through the leftover anxiety as the water slowly engulfed her body.

"It was a dream, only a dream," she whispered to herself.

It was a nightmare!

Thinking back on what her dream mind had created, she wasn't surprised her psyche had placed the man at the coffee shop and Orion as the same person, what with the last message of his that she'd read.

"Maybe I need to stop online dating," she whispered as the burning in her ankle became negligible and the heat of the water slowly relaxed her tense muscles. Sighing, she turned the water off and leaned back against the tub. She knew she should start trying to remove the jewelry, but convinced herself it would be best to let it soak as long as possible. After all, she did not want to tear her skin again.

Closing her eyes, she tried to focus on Terrian, but found it difficult to do so. Every time she would pull the image of his photo into her mind, it would quickly be replaced with Orion's. Frustrated, she elected to think of something, anything else, and before she knew it, she fell asleep.

Arwen! Wake up!

The sound of someone calling her name had her blinking her eyes open. "In the bathroom!" she called out, wondering who had called out to her. Nobody responded, and when she shivered, she realized she was lying in cold water. "How long have I been in here?"

Groaning, she stood up and got out, quickly drying herself and throwing on her robe. Yanking out the stopper on the tub, she trotted out of the bathroom and into her living room. "Hello!" she called out. No reply. "Who's there?" she called again, looking around.

Still no reply.

Confused, she checked her front door, only to find it locked and dead-bolted. How strange.

Shaking her head to rid herself of the fluff that still seemed to linger from her impromptu nap, she went into the kitchen and poured some milk into a pan on the stove. "I think I need some hot chocolate."

As she turned to pour out the hot chocolate, a low thrumming in her ankle made her look down. "No!" The anklet was gone. In its place were raised criss-crossed welts exactly where the metal had been. "No, no, no!" Running back into the bathroom, she checked the tub. The water was gone and at first she didn't see anything. Then, she spotted it. Sitting near the stopper, was a piece of golden metal. Grasping it, she yanked it up and stared, knowing immediately that it was the clasp of the anklet.

"It dissolved?" she gasped, looking at it. She had showered every day with it on and would never have guessed that the metal would disintegrate like that. Whimpering at the loss of such a beautiful piece of jewelry, she placed the clasp, the only part of it left, on the counter and went back to fix her drink. Once the chocolate was mixed with the milk, she added an equal amount of vodka.

Slouching into her chair, she sipped at the drink. When had this day gone wrong? It had started out okay, but somewhere along the way, it went all wonky. Sighing, she gulped the last of her hot chocolate and stared across the room at her computer. A long thrum settled through her ankle and she stared at it absentmindedly. She supposed her ankle would have some aftereffects of her allergy. Looking back up at the computer, next thing she knew she was in front of it, turning it on.

A small voice in the back of her head said this was not like her, but while she acknowledged that was true, she could not stop herself. "Twenty-two new emails," she muttered as she watched them fall into folders. IDS had seven. Her eyes lit up and she quickly clicked the folder.

You have a new message from AttractivelyAgile
You have a new message from AttractivelyAgile
You have a new message from AttractivelyAgile
You have a new message from AttractivelyAgile
You have a new message from AttractivelyAgile
You have a new message from CuriousityLemmings
You have mail from DaringlyGauche

She blinked at the messages. The last one was from earlier and she would look at it in a minute, but her heart sped up as she saw the five messages from Orion. It did a backflip as she saw the message from Terrian.

"Yes," she whispered in relief, opening it up.

Arwen,

> *That is a beautiful name. So, you live in a library as well? Well, that is wonderful to hear. Though maybe not for you. It can be a bit taxing. I thought it would be nice to tell you a little more about myself, if that would be acceptable to you. If not, read no further.*

> *I am a rather large sports enthusiast and wish I could spend more time engaged in them rather than watching. My favorites are wind surfing and tree skiffing. Do not spread this around, but I also have a deep love for animals. My mount Abriethon has been with me for a few decades and I swear he knows me*

71

better than anyone else. I also raise Dipthan Kivees, somewhat similar to the Orenean Brevs, but my mother and I have been striving to breed the perfect corg with a more malleable temper.

Have you ever jumped dimensions before? I did when I was much younger. Unfortunately, I found it did not bode well for my temperament, so I stopped. My brothers Caifu and Stero spent a couple centuries doing it and it never affected them, though, so it might just be me. My youngest brother, Zenun, jumped once but found the shift too painful. He stayed in the Anjolan Sphere for fifty years before he was killed accidentally. We tried to get him to come back home before then, but he stubbornly refused.

I was sorry to hear you lost your mother. Losing one's parent must be a dreadful experience. My mother has just passed her millennial birthday and is stronger than ever. My father is close to his bimillenial. I am quite young at only 745 years. Within my direct family, I have two older brothers and seven younger. There are many other relations who I will not mention, as to do so would take far too much space.

Besides the books I have read, I am unfamiliar with your particular dimension. Would you be willing to tell me about it? Or anything you wish to write about. I would just like to get to know you better.

Looking forward to your next message,

Terrian

All her excitement about his message died as Ari read it. What was wrong with the men from IDS? Were they clinically insane? Maybe they were trapped in a mental ward somewhere and used this as their way to get to know people? Disappointed, her finger hovered over the delete button. Her ankle stung lightly, and she reached down to rub it. Maybe she would delete it later.

Sighing, she looked at the unread messages from the other two sites. After deleting all of them, she glanced at DaringlyGauche's. His message was innocuous and rather boring, but considering how disappointed she was, she barely noticed. Clicking on the link to view his profile, she looked at Orion's messages.

Maybe she should reply to let him know she had received them but wasn't interested. He might think she hadn't gotten them. He was weird enough. It might never have crossed his mind that someone would not be interested in him.

Glancing at her browser, she saw only ten percent of Gauche's profile had downloaded, so she opened Orion's oldest message.

Corruptible,

Are you ignoring me? It won't last for long, beautiful lady. I doubt you can resist my charms.

Orion

Snorting, she went on to read the next.

Corruptible,

Respond immediately.

Orion

…and the next.

Write back now!
Orion

…and the next.

If I do not hear back soon, I will be greatly displeased. And, pet, you do not want me to be displeased.
Orion

A shiver went down her spine at the fourth message. Pet? That was what he had called her in her nightmare. How could she have known he would call her that?

Gulping, she opened his last message.

Your master sends you a flower, and you do not even deign to acknowledge its existence? That is very bad behavior. Never fear. I still plan to collect you and turn you into the perfect pet. Your insolence will cost you at first.

I must say, it does warm my heart that you have placed it where you sleep. Dream of me, pet.

Orion

"Oh, no. No, no, no, no," she murmured to herself, reading and then re-reading the last message. Her eyes slanted toward her bedroom where the flower was and she became aware of a stinging pain in her ankle.

Jumping up, she ran into the bedroom and grabbed the vase, letting out a little scream as the stinging pain became unimaginable agony. Gasping, she kept her hand around the vase and limped out into her living room, opened her front door, and tossed the flower— vase and all—out into the small garbage can nearby. After slamming the top down on it, she limped back into her apartment, confused when she realized her ankle no longer hurt.

It was still thrumming, something it had been doing since she got out of the bathtub, but the pain was mostly gone.

"Weird," she whispered as she deleted all of Orion's messages as well as the one from DaringlyGauche. When her finger went to delete Terrian's message, her ankle throbbed twice making her think twice about it. "I can delete it later."

Closing down DaringlyGauche's profile without even looking at it, she shut her computer down and collapsed into her chair. Something strange was going on. Before she could figure it out, her phone began to ring.

Moaning, because she really did not want to talk to anyone, she answered it. "Yes?"

"Arwen, I am sure your mother taught you to answer the phone nicer than that." Abigail's voice was stern and yet amused.

"Hey, Abigail. Sorry. It has been a really weird, disturbing day."

"Disturbing, how?" Her grandmother's concerned tone made her smile. She would have laughed at it if it weren't for the fact she was a little weirded out by current events.

"It is hard to explain," Ari sighed. "In the last week, so many things have happened, and at first, I thought they were odd, but until today I never assumed they might be connected." Having her grandmother call her once, let alone three times in the same week just added to it.

"Arwen Maria Reynolds, tell me what is going on.

Maybe my psychic was more right that we thought."

"Okay, well, I haven't even begun to process it yet, but maybe by talking about it, I can put the pieces together."

Leaning back, she started to tell Abigail about her week. "It all started a couple days after Jane had me sign up for some online dating services. I was getting weird power fluctuations both here and at work, one of the services sent me a gift, and I got contacted by a really weird guy."

"Wait," Abigail interrupted. "What gift did this online dating service send you? I wasn't aware they did that."

"It was a beautiful piece of jewelry. An anklet." Ari blushed as she prepared to tell the rest. "Strangely enough, it seemed to fit my ankle perfectly, and once it was on, I could not remove it."

"Oh, Lord," Abigail muttered.

Ari continued as she needed to get all the pieces out before she forgot. "Yesterday, I went out for coffee with some friends, and the barista brought me one from a stranger. I didn't get a good look at him, but he looked rich, and something about him was off, so I ended up throwing the coffee away. But that wasn't the weird part."

"What was the weird part?"

"I got a new message from that weird guy, and his postscript asked me if I liked chocolate in my coffee. Abigail, the barista brought me a white chocolate latte."

Abigail inhaled sharply, but did not interrupt.

"Added to that, these guys keep acting as though they are from some different world—you know, as if they were in some role-playing game. Last night, I got a decent message from what looked and sounded like a decent guy. Then today happened."

Her grandmother let out a whoosh of air. "Well, come on, Arwen. Let me hear about today so we can figure this thing out."

Grimacing, Ari told her grandmother about the entire day—about her ankle hurting and the strange flower, about Terrian and his disappointing message, and lastly about the piece of jewelry disintegrating in her bath. The only thing she held back was the bad dreams.

"Arwen, you say the anklet disintegrated?"

"Yes. The only thing left after my bath was the clasp."

Abigail sighed and muttered under her breath something that sounded like, "I told Destra she needed to tell you, but oh, no! She wanted to keep it all a big secret." Her voice rose and she spoke into the phone again. "Arwen, what was the name of this online dating service?"

"Oh, the Interdimensional Dating Service. It—" She stopped as Abigail let out a shout.

"NO!"

Surprised at the outburst, Ari sat and chewed on her lip, wondering why her grandmother would be so upset.

"Arwen, tell me something. When you brought up their website, is that when the flashing of your screen started?"

Frowning, Ari started to shake her head no, but then realized, "Actually, yes I think it was."

Groaning, her grandmother said something in a language Ari did not understand. "Arwen, I want you to listen to me closely. I cannot say everything I wish as this line is too open, but honey, you entered into something you really should not be dealing with."

"But Jane said her friends found their husbands through it." Ari's voice trailed off as she realized she had never told Jane the actual name of the website.

"Somehow I doubt they used that particular site." Abigail snorted. "Arwen, have you had any strange dreams?"

Sitting up straight, Ari nodded, before finally saying, "Yes," in nothing but a whisper.

"Before or after the jewelry?"

"After. Actually they came last night and again today."

"Arwen, I am sending you a picture. Take a look and tell me if it looks familiar. My line is about to go out, but I will call you later on to find out."

Without another word, the line was cut.

Placing her phone on the coffee table, Arwen glanced around her room, suddenly feeling afraid. What was going on? Her grandmother seemed to think it was bad. *"You entered into something you really should not be dealing with."* Well, how was she supposed to know?

Looking down, she was surprised to find herself rubbing her ankle. "Why do I do that?"

Groaning, she stood up and made sure her door was locked. As a precaution, she placed her high-backed chair in front of it and under the knob. She felt a little stupid, but not feeling comfortable in her own place was unnerving her, not to mention she was almost afraid to go back into her bedroom.

The buzz from her phone made her jump and

scrambling across the room, she picked it up. It was a picture from Abigail. The title said *Shift Bracelet*. Pulling it up, her eyes zeroed in on the small image. Almost at once, her breath started coming in short, quick pants, and her heart sped up.

Staring back at her was a picture of a wrist with a series of red criss-crossed welts upon it in a beautiful design. If she did not know already, she would have assumed they were a tat of some sort.

But she did know. Looking down, she stared at her own ankle. The design was different, but there was no denying that the owner of that design had worn the same kind of jewelry she had.

What had she gotten herself into?

Chapter Six - *Interdimensional Shift*

The next morning, Ari slowly dragged her eyes open, groaning at how much energy it took. Blinking, she was surprised at first to find herself sitting in her living room and not in her bed.

Then she remembered.

Gulping, she winced at her sore throat as her eyes darted over to her bedroom door. Something had changed, and even though she had thrown out the offensive flower, her bedroom no longer seemed safe. Not that her living room was that much safer, but her only other choice was to call one of her sisters and ask if she could bunk on their couch for the night.

She did not want to field the questions that would have come from that.

Slowly standing up, she moaned. She felt horrible. Her muscles ached, her throat felt like sandpaper, and her eyes burned. A small part of her, the part that seemed to find humor in the oddest moments was amused that at least the burn had moved from her ankle. The rest of her was not so pleased.

Limping into her bathroom, she took a hot shower, which just seemed to make all the achiness worse. "I've never been sick a day from work," she mumbled to her blotchy complexion in the bathroom mirror. "Today will not be the first."

As she hobbled into her bedroom, trying to ignore

the way the hairs on the back of her neck stood up the second she passed the threshold, her closet seemed awfully far away. And with each step, it seemed further and further. Moaning, she felt as though she could not take another step and crumpled to the floor.

"I'm not sick," she mumbled through dry lips. Her body was still aware she was in her bedroom, and before she knew it, she had crawled out of it into the living room, collapsing in front of the sofa.

"I can't move," she muttered to nobody as she laid there. She could not remember ever getting ill. Jane and Cory both had suffered from the flu, chicken pox, as well as allergies. She, however, had seemed to escape when those maladies came calling. "I guess I was due," she said in a nasally voice.

Reaching for her phone, she quickly dialed her boss's office line. Just holding the phone to her ear seemed to take all of her energy. When her message was finished, she let the phone drop then allowed her body to drop as well and quickly fell asleep.

When she woke up, she felt worse. Tears poured from her eyes as she pulled herself up onto all fours and made her way to the kitchen. Looking up at the very high countertops, she knew coffee was not going to happen. Whimpering made her wince from the pain in her throat and more tears escaped. She turned around and hobbled back to the living room, pulling up part way onto the chair.

Leaning her head down on the leather seat, she closed her eyes and drifted.

"That's good, pet. Yes, don't fight it. Your body is going through the shift. Soon you will be with me always."

Ari's eyes sprang open at the sound of Orion's voice. Her ankle burned and every muscle in her body seemed to twitch as she looked around the room, almost expecting to see the man with red eyes.

Maybe this illness had been coming on for a while. It would make the delusions she seemed to be having make more sense. Letting out another whimper, her eyes started to close again.

"Shh, pet. Just let yourself fall asleep. It will make the shift easier." She shivered as a cool finger drifted across her cheek. *"When you awaken there is much to be done, so get your rest now."*

Her ankle fizzled at his touch, and yet something in his voice made her want to obey him. As the muscles within her body relaxed, she felt herself drift further toward darkness, toward him.

"Good little pet."

Every muscle tensed as a loud blaring noise made her eyes snap open. Looking around, she realized she was still in her living room, and the sound that woke her was her phone.

Groaning, she reached for it, but it was so far away. It would take so much energy to reach it.

"That's right, pet," he whispered in her ear. *"Ignore the sound. Go back to sleep."*

Whimpering, she forced herself to reach further.

His voice hardened. *"No, pet. Stop. Go to sleep."*

Her ankle once again flashed with pain, but it gave her enough energy to lunge toward the phone, toppling over on top of it.

"Hello?" she yawned as she opened it.

"Arwen?"

"Yes," she muttered, almost immediately feeling

herself drift again.

"Arwen Maria Reynolds! Snap out of it!" Abigail's voice demanded through the phone.

"Wha—?" she gasped, sitting up straight, blinking her eyes open. Why did she feel drugged?

"Arwen, are you listening to me?"

Her head felt strange, as though stuffed with cotton balls. Ari shook her head violently to try and clear it. "Yes, Abigail, I am listening. I'm sick today and can't concentrate."

"No, Arwen, you are not sick. Well, you are, but it isn't a malady you have ever heard of. Tell me, have you seen Orion again?"

Ari felt that was a strange question, but yawned. "Yeah, he keeps calling me his pet and telling me to relax and rest." It sounded like good advice. She was so tired. Leaning over, she laid her head on the floor as she kept the phone to her ear. It took too much energy to sit up.

"Good pet. Let it go." As she closed her eyes, she felt his fingers drift down her arm. *"Just sleep, pet. Sleep."*

"ARWEN!"

Groaning, Ari blinked her eyes open again. "I can't," she mumbled into the phone. "Too much energy to stay awake."

"Arwen, listen to me. This is not going to make a lot of sense, but you are shifting from one dimension to another, dearest. That is why you feel so ill. You must fight it, Arwen. Do you hear me? You must fight the desire to sleep. You must fight his encouragement!"

The words made no sense, and Ari moaned softly, unable to say anything. All she really felt was something soft drifting up and down her arm and a deep thrum within her reacting to it.

"That's a good pet. Turn off the phone. Come on, pet. Turn off the phone."

Yawning, her finger reached over to cut off the line. Before she could, her grandmother yelled something she could not understand. At the same time, fire lit up her leg and screaming, she sat up, rubbing at the flames she could not see.

She felt a flash of anger, and then all she could hear was the sound of her own breathing.

"Arwen?"

Looking at her hand, she pulled the phone up to her ear. "Yeah, I'm still here. My leg hurts."

"I know it does. I needed to do something to get the bastard away from you. I need you to do something for me, Arwen, and it is going to sound very strange. Will you do it?"

"Sure, Abigail," she said with a yawn. Nothing her grandmother could suggest would be any odder than what her last week had been like.

"Good, I want you to stand up."

Snorting, Ari somehow forced herself onto her feet. The burning in her leg was still there but had dimmed somewhat. "Okay, I'm standing, but I don't know how long it will last."

"Are you dressed?"

Ari looked down. "Nope."

"Damn. Keep the phone with you, go into your room, and put on the first thing your hand touches. I'm coming, Arwen. It's just taking longer than I would wish. Now, go get dressed."

Stumbling into her bedroom, she pulled on a pair

of shorts and a T-shirt and slipped her feet into a pair of bunny slippers. "Okay," she yawned. "I'm dressed."

"Good. Now, grab your keys, go to your car, and drive over to Cory's."

Frowning, Ari glanced at her front door. It seemed so insurmountable. "I don't think that is a good idea. I can barely walk."

"Ari, you need to get out of your apartment. Go now!"

Abigail called her by her nickname; the surprise of it pulled her out of her stupor. Focusing intently on her goal, she grabbed her keys and somehow made it out of her apartment to her car without falling down. By the time she fell into the driver's seat, though, she felt nauseated. "I don't feel good," she moaned into the phone.

"I know, Arwen, and I will help, but we need to get you to Cory's house. Can you drive?"

"I'll try." Placing the phone on speaker and putting it in the passenger seat, she started the car and backed up, focusing intently on the road. She never realized it curved so much nor that it was so dark.

"Pull over, pet. You are too tired to drive. Ignore the phone. Pull over and sleep. I will help." His breath washed over her ear and she shivered, biting her lip.

"Orion, you bastard!" Abigail yelled from her phone. "Arwen, try to ignore him! Just focus on the road, on Cory. Come on, you can get to Cory. Once you get to her house, you can sleep all you want."

Blinking her eyes open, once again the dry gray of the road met her gaze, and she pushed a little harder on the gas pedal.

"Stop right now, pet. You are putting yourself and

others in danger. You don't want to kill anyone, do you?" He stroked her jaw softly.

"No," she moaned. She didn't want to kill anyone and he was right. If she continued driving, she might cause an accident. Glancing to her right, she pulled into a parking lot. "Must sleep," she murmured.

"Arwen, no!" Abigail yelled, but this time Ari was too far gone to reply. She could hear her grandmother and Orion, but could respond to neither. An odd thought drifted through her mind. It seemed strange that her grandmother and her delusion were talking to one another. Before she could truly grasp onto the thought, it left.

"Orion, you will not get your hands on my granddaughter. Go back to the nether realm you came from!"

He laughed coldly. "You never learn, do you Abigail? I always get what I want. Always. And Arwen will make a perfect replacement slave. My last one was not able to handle the shift well. She only lasted two years in my realm. Arwen, however—"

"It will be the same!" Abigail snapped. "You will kill Arwen just as you did her!" She snarled the last few words making him chuckle.

"Oh, she is still alive. I never kill my pets. She just does not function." He chuckled again. "Arwen will be much hardier. There is magic within her, Abigail. I can feel it. Once she is fully my slave, I will teach her to use it." He reached out and stroked the cheek of the girl who would soon be his. "Give up, Abigail. She is mine."

"NEVER!" she screamed.

Ari felt his fingers stroke her cheek and her arm.

"Sleep, pet. This will all be over soon." And unable to deny him, she did.

****

Ari's body ached, from the tips of her toes to the tips of the hair on her head. She didn't even know hair could hurt. Wasn't it supposed to be dead? Moaning, she tried to open her eyes, but they were so heavy. What was going on?

Taking a deep breath to steady herself, she stopped breathing as cold, damp air settled in her lungs. Was it raining again? If so, what was she doing outside?

Now what was going on? Once again, she tried to remember where she was before she fell asleep, but the memories were vague, unsettling...distant. Almost as though they were the memories of someone else.

"Awake, pet." The deep voice rattled through her body awakening all her nerve endings. She felt very itchy and uncomfortable all of a sudden.

Forcing her eyes open, she groaned at the darkness that encircled her. "Am I dreaming again?" she mumbled. While she could not quite draw the dream into memory, she had a distinct memory that she'd had a dream once about being in a cold dark room with a strange man.

"Ah, she is awake," he crooned softly.

As her body stiffened and she sat up, she became aware of the fact she was sitting on cold stone and her body felt as if it had been through a wringer. "Who's there?" she managed to get through her lips, even though she instinctively knew it was somebody important.

A deep cold chuckle encircled her, making her feel at home and yet abandoned at the same time. It was a very disconcerting mixture. "The shift has made you somewhat forgetful, pet? No matter. You will soon remember." The sound of a match being struck and the sight of fire flashing into the air caught her attention, and she turned toward it. Standing a few feet away was a man who looked familiar, holding the flame. He was wearing dark pants and a dark button-down shirt.

He lit a candle with the match and turned toward her, holding the candle above his head so she could not see his face. She had seen this before. She knew she had. What did it mean? Before she could try to figure it out, he crouched down in front of her and took hold of her chin. "Pet, you are mine. You will refer to me as Master. Understand?"

As she went to nod her head, her ankle sizzled making her hiss in pain. Reaching out, her hands settled on top of skin that was slightly raised in an odd, crisscross design. Once again, her memory tugged at her consciousness. There was something about this place, this person that she needed to remember. But what?

He tightened his hold on her chin. "Pet, answer me. What do you call me?" His voice had intensified, and her body seemed to thrum with each syllable. Instinctively she knew that to deny him would cause her pain, and she did not want that. Plus, something within her told her to follow this man—that this was what she was born to do.

As she sat looking at him, his words continued to thrum through her, tightening her chest the longer she held out. Her ability to breathe became hindered and panic built within her. "Master," she whimpered, relieved when her chest loosened and she could breathe again.

A cold chuckle came from his chest. "Very good, pet." Standing up, he pulled her roughly to her feet. "I am your master. You are my pet. Above all, you are my slave. Do you accept your master's enslavement, pet?" The power within his question robbed her of any control. Her lips formed the word yes, while her body did not allow her to vocalize it.

He pulled the candle down so she could see his face, and she could feel the blood drain out of her face as she looked into his cold red eyes. "Pet, you will obey and answer your master. Or you will pay for it." He leaned in. "And you are already due for several punishments. Do not make it worse on yourself. Answer me. Do you accept your enslavement to me, your master?"

Once again, the syllables started to thrum through her, and her chest began to tighten. Not wanting to be short of breath again, she shouted out, "Ye—" but before she could complete the word, it felt as though her ankle burst into flames. "No!" she screamed, yanking from his grasp and dropping down to rub at the pain.

A large roar filled the air, and she looked up, horrified to see him glaring at her. "No?" he hissed. "You think you can say no to your master, pet?" A cold hard smile crossed his face. "Fine. Until you are ready to obey, I will force you." Grabbing her by the hair, he turned, dragging her behind him.

"Wait!" she screeched, grabbing for her hair to stop him from pulling it out. Her knees dragged along the rough stone floor and the combined pain of her ankle and head made everything sharper. She wanted to tell him she couldn't stop the scream earlier because of the pain, that she hadn't meant to say no to him. But he was causing her even more pain, and she was beginning to feel pissed off. The shakiness she had felt when she awakened seemed to have disappeared, replaced with pure anger.

"Stop!" she screamed. He ignored her, tightening his hold on her hair and pulling her faster. Her anger grew as did the pain in her ankle until she wasn't sure whether the pain fed the anger or the anger fed the pain. "You ugly red-eyed freak! Let me go!" Reaching up, she grabbed onto his hand and squeezed.

He let out a roar, surprising her. He sounded like a wild animal. At the same time, he released her hair and jumped a few feet away. As she massaged her head where the hair had been yanked, she watched him. He held the hand she had squeezed in his other as though she had crushed it or something.

"Oh, don't be a big baby!" she snapped at the small whimpers that fell from his lips.

His eyes flashed to hers, and she started crawling backwards as fast as her hands and butt would take her. He bared his teeth at her, and a small guttural growl left his throat. As if that wasn't scary enough, his red eyes glowed.

"What the hell are you?" she gasped, still not understanding where she was, but knowing logically none of this was normal.

His growl paused and he chuckled unkindly. "You will learn, pet. In the meantime, enjoy your cell. Until you accept your enslavement, you will not leave it." Without another word, he dropped the candle and as it hit the floor the flame snuffed out, immediately leaving her in total darkness.

She froze in fear, unable to see a thing. As the sound of his boots made a familiar *c-clap, c-clap, c-clap* along the stone, it became quieter and quieter. He was leaving. Gulping, she barely recognized the fact before the sound of a rusty metal door opened and closed, the slam of it jarring her out of her stupor.

Okay, where was she, and why was she here? Also, where had she come from? Unthinking, she lay her forehead in the palm of her right hand while resting her elbow on her knee. She wrapped her left palm on her left ankle. Almost immediately, the fog lifted. "Oh, I am…" As she spoke, her hands moved from her skin and just like that, her memory dulled. "Crap!" She had almost known who she was.

Whimpering, she moved her hands out from her body trying to find something besides cold hard floor. In her immediate vicinity, there was nothing. Knowing there had to be a wall to lean against, she turned over onto her hands and raw knees and moved slowly in one direction and felt out ahead of her with each move, waiting for the wall that had to exist.

As she crawled, she tried to bring back the memory she had barely grasped before it disappeared. It had been so clear and then it was gone.

After several minutes of crawling and not finding anything, she became frustrated. "There has to be a wall somewhere," she grumbled, sitting down for a few minutes. Her wrists hurt from crawling on them as did her knees. Obviously, she wasn't used to this kind of thing. So, she could not have been here long, right?

Sighing, she crossed her legs and rested her elbows on her knees, cupping her chin in her hands. "So, I'm stuck in the darkness with some red-eyed freak who calls himself my master." She sighed. She was positive she could not have signed up for this. It didn't seem like her, even if she wasn't sure who she was.

Her left ankle tingled, and she removed her left hand from her chin to rub it. Immediately the fog cleared from her mind again. She gasped, her head snapping back, and the fog came back. "Wait." The first time it happened, she was holding her ankle and her forehead. This time she was holding her chin and her ankle.

"Well, that's just stupid," she snorted, shaking her head. There was no way placing her hand on her ankle would magically lift her mental block. "Magic doesn't exist, except in fairytales."

Taking a deep breath, she lowered her chin onto her right hand and dabbled her left hand over her left ankle. It wouldn't hurt just to lay it on her ankle just to see, she thought, scoffing at herself for even thinking something so stupid. The longer she sat there though, the less stupid it sounded. She was trapped in a seemingly endless blackness by some red-eyed weirdo. Maybe there was something to this strange hand on her ankle thing.

Taking a deep breath, she placed one finger on the ankle.

Nothing.

Chuckling at her silliness, as well as feeling just a slight bit of disappointment, she placed her full palm down. Immediately, the fog lifted, and she could see a room. It was small, oval, and had nothing in it except an inlaid wooden floor that was placed in a very intricate design. At the same moment, the design in another form came to mind. "The jewelry box," she whispered. Her head jerked back and the fog once again settled.

"Oh, for heaven's sake!" she snapped and once again laid her chin in her hand. This would get old. The only way to access her memories was to sit like this? A strange thought that these were not memories went through her mind, but she pushed it right out again. How else could she be seeing it so clearly if it wasn't a memory? Before she could settle into any more anger, once again she was in that room, the design was glowing now and someone was chanting something…a name.

Arwen…

That was an odd name.

Arwen…

There it was again. She looked around, this time seeing two women sitting outside the room, their hands reaching toward the door, the name Arwen falling from their lips along with other words and grunts that made no sense whatsoever.

She cocked her head as she realized she knew the two women. One was her sister, Cory. The other was… Abigail! And yet, not Abigail. It looked like Abigail would have looked in her thirties rather than in her nineties. As if all her memories felt it was okay to come out all of a sudden, she remembered being sick, so sick, and Abigail telling her to hold on, and that she needed to get to Cory. "Yes, I needed to get to Cory," she whispered, remembering how adamant her grandmother had been.

Something had stopped her. A voice. *Just sleep, pet. Sleep.* As the words came to her, her ankle sizzled in pain, and memories of the other times her ankle had erupted into pain came to her. Every time she had something to do with him, with Orion, her ankle had reacted. "Oh my," she whispered, realizing whatever the anklet had done to her, it had been trying to help her fight off Orion. Or had it? Maybe it had actually come from him rather than the Interdimensional Dating Service?

Or was he the Interdimensional Dating Service? She gulped at the thought and wondered how many women he had captured in this game he was playing.

"Arwen!"

This time the voices sounded more natural, as though they were talking to her. Figuring she might as well see if they would respond, she whispered, "Yes?"

"Oh, Arwen, we were afraid we would not be able to reach you! Has he convinced you to accept his enslavement yet?"

How did they know? Shaking her head because she could ask them later, she said, "No, and he was really angry about it. Weird things are going on though. Like why when I touch my ankle and my face..." she stopped and flushed a little at the stupidity she was about to say.

"I will explain when you get back. You must come back, Arwen. You need to come back to this dimension before you become too accustomed to his. Can you do that?"

Could she do that? What the hell? She wasn't even sure how she had got here in the first place. "You have got to be kidding me."

Cory's laugh made her relax a bit. If her sister could still laugh, things must not be too bad. Of course, there was also the possibility she was insane and locked up in a room somewhere. She would not discount that option just yet.

"Ari, can you see the room? The room with the design in the middle?"

Ari's thoughts immediately flipped back to that first room she saw. "Yes."

"Good, focus on it. Do not take your eyes off the design. I know this sounds strange, but see yourself in that room. Concentrate on it. Ignore everything else."

"Yes, Arwen," Abigail interrupted. "Ignore everything. Including him and I assure you he will come back as soon as he realizes you are in danger of leaving. He cannot touch you while you are not fully in his realm."

"But he already touched me…several times," Ari cried out in panic.

"That was when you were in his realm. The more you focus on the design, the more you will drift between them. No matter what happens, focus on that design. Your body will become tired, so tired you won't think you'll be able to remain awake. No matter what, do not lose sight of that design. Do you understand?"

"Yes, Abigail. The design is in my mind."

"Good. Cory and I will help."

Once again, they started chanting words and grunts she did not understand. As the room and design came into clearer focus, she became aware of a loud sound coming closer and closer. "Something is coming!" she hissed, trying to not lose sight of the design while trying to look around to see if she could see anything.

"Ignore him, Arwen. Just focus!"

Whimpering, she continued to focus on the room with the wooden floor, ever aware that the sound she heard as it became louder was the *c-clap* of his boots on the stone. He was running in her direction. Her body started to shake as she heard the *BAM!* as the iron door slammed open and the sound of his boots as he dashed toward her.

"STOP!" he yelled in a loud snarl.

A part of her almost did, but Cory and Abigail shouted for her to continue. Her body, shaking with the energy it took to focus clearly on the room and not defend herself, was becoming very tired very fast.

"Pet, stop what you are doing," he said in a cold purr right into her ear. She squeaked, but continued to focus. "They are stealing you from me, pet. I will not stand for this!" Something brushed past her arm, and she gasped at how cold it felt but continued to focus. Her ankle thrummed strongly and by focusing on that, it seemed easier to focus on the design and the room.

He let out a loud roar as the room and design became more intense and seemed to get larger. "*Pet, you have not escaped me,*" he said, his voice becoming softer as though further away. "*I will come get you and next time, you will be punished immediately for your disobedience. Do yourself a favor, pet. Turn back now to me. If you do, your punishment will be far less than it will be if you continue to follow that evil woman!*"

Fear struck at her chest at the thought of what punishment he might give her. Almost automatically, she went to turn her head to look at him. Her ankle burned intensely, making her scream, as the room suddenly reached up and grabbed her, and she tumbled into it, straight toward the hard floor. Screaming again, she wrapped her arms over her head to protect it and waited for the feeling of the hard ground to hit her.

Chapter Seven - *Interdimensional Culpability*

The sound of water running brought Ari around. Blinking, she tried to figure out where she was. Things seemed brighter, not as sinister. Sitting up, she looked at blank walls. Her brain still felt fuzzy, but she was at least able to sit up without feeling nauseated. It took only one glance to find she was lying on a thin mattress in a small oval room.

The floor was covered with inlaid wood in a design that looked familiar to her, but as the mattress covered part of it, she could not call it to mind. A door opened and she looked up, surprised by the person who entered. "Cory?"

Smiling, her sister nodded. "How do you feel, sis?"

Moving her head from side to side, Ari shrugged. "Still a little foggy, but I don't seem to be aching as much."

"Good. Good thing we found you when we did," she sighed, sitting on the floor next to the mattress. "We were almost too late. That bastard," she muttered under her breath.

Frowning, Ari laid back down, resting her head, which was slightly pounding. "What happened?" It all seemed like a dream, and she half expected Cory to explain she missed her date with Jay because she became ill. That would make everything make sense to her.

"Well," she said quietly. "The short description is you accidentally contacted a being from another dimension who has legal claim to certain women in our family, and he tried to take you."

Blinking again, Ari stared at her sister, sure she could not have heard what came out of her mouth. Closing her eyes, she took a deep breath and opened them again. Her big sister snickered and winked at her. "Yeah, it is a lot to take in, isn't it?"

"That's putting it lightly," she responded dryly. "When do I wake up?"

Laughing, Cory patted her arm. "Unfortunately you are awake, little sister. Abigail will be here within a day or two, and she will help us figure out a way around all of this."

Frowning, Ari sat up again. "Are you telling me everything that happened actually happened?"

"Yep. And you only know a tiny part of it." Turning, she placed a hand on Ari's left ankle, which gave out a soft hum making her jump. "I remember the first time I saw Mom's," she said quietly. "It was just before my sixteenth birthday, and I wanted to know where she got it because I wanted one, too." Chuckling, she removed her hand and shrugged. "She was never one to tell lies and before I knew it, explained everything to me."

She snorted. "Oh, Ari, wait until you hear the story. You will be sure the whole fucking world has turned upside down." Standing up, she held a hand out to help Ari to her feet. Ari took it hesitantly. "So, the moment I heard what that thing actually meant, I changed my mind and did not want it. Unfortunately, nobody ever told you about it so you were not prepared."

Cory picked up the small mattress. "I'll be right back. Whatever you do, don't leave this room."

Ordinarily, Ari would make some sarcastic comment back, but considering the last few days, she was not feeling like herself. This room had rescued her from Orion, and she was actually afraid to leave it. Hell, she was afraid to stay in it, but the fear of doing anything at the moment caused her to freeze and stand still over the design.

While she waited for her sister, Ari looked down. There was that design again, and this time she clearly recognized it as the one on the jewelry box. Glancing down at her ankle, she shook her head. What had she gotten herself in to? In the last week, she had signed up for dating sites, been burned by a strange piece of jewelry, become stalked by a red-eyed weirdo, crossed some sort of strange barrier into another dimension, and then been sucked back into her own.

"I must be insane," she muttered.

Laughing, Cory reappeared, toting two folding chairs. "Can't bring much in here as only a few things have been designated for it, but at least this way we can sit down." She handed her sister one of them and they both opened the chairs and sat down at the same time.

"Cory, I think I'm losing it." That was it. She was going crazy. That was the only logical explanation.

Cory's angular face filled with compassion. "I know this is a lot to take in, Ari, but everything that happened to you did actually happen." The emphasis on the last three words did not make Ari feel any better.

"But that's impossible!" she spluttered. "Magic and different dimensions don't exist!" A part of her recognized that she sounded like a petulant child, but she did not care. She just wanted to go back to being blissfully unaware of such things. "When does it go away?"

Wincing, Cory turned and looked around—anywhere but at her little sister. "It doesn't, Arwen. Once you know, it just becomes more pronounced. You start recognizing the signs everywhere." She sighed. "If Destra had explained those things to you, then you would have seen that dating site for what it was."

"Jane knows too?" Ari guessed.

Snorting, Cory shook her head. "She doesn't want to accept it and refused to believe it was anything but a fairytale when Mom told her. Maybe that was why Destra didn't tell you."

Nodding, Ari stared at the design on the floor. "What does this mean?" she asked, pointing at it.

"I'll have Abigail explain it. To be honest, I don't truly understand. I learned enough to recognize the signs of paranormal activity, and how to stay away from them, but never delved deeply into it. I just didn't want to know."

The two sisters sat lost in thought for a while, but Ari was having trouble with the silence. It reminded her too much of the blackness she just escaped. "So, where is Abigail that it's taking her so long to get here?"

Smirking, Cory chuckled. "In her own dimension."

Blinking Ari stared at her sister. Surely, she could not have heard correctly. "Pardon?"

"Does it really surprise you to hear Abigail isn't from here, Ari? After everything you've gone through over the last few days?" Seeing Ari's blank look, she grimaced. "Okay, here is the long and short of it. Abigail is from a parallel dimension. She used to be a dimension jumper, going back and forth at will, but that stopped about seventy years ago."

Ari almost asked what happened seventy years ago, but was afraid it would mean she truly was insane.

"See, she had an affair with a man from a bicollandrial dimension and did not find out she was pregnant until way after the affair. By that time, she was visiting ours. She wasn't sure how dimension jumping would affect the pregnancy, so she elected to stay here for eleven months until Destra was born."

"Eleven months?" Ari asked confused. "Pregnancies only last nine."

"In our dimension," Cory nodded. "Not in hers.

"I guess the birth of Destra really threw her for a loop, and she stayed here for twenty more years, until her daughter was able to manage for herself and then left. She stayed in touch just like she does with us, through phone calls, letters, and packages. But she did not come back until the day Destra received a piece of jewelry—a bracelet that seared her flesh and left a design behind." Cory nodded toward Ari's ankle. "Just like that one.

"She had to come back to visit, explain to Destra what she was and what the design meant. She also had to warn her that men from other dimensions would contact her now that she had been marked." Cory blew out a breath. "Unfortunately, Abigail was a hair too late. Mom had already fallen in love with a man who turned out to be from a different dimension. I was born a year later."

"Oh," Ari gasped. She always wondered who their fathers were.

Cory shrugged. "Mom did not want us to have to

deal with dimension jumping and magic so she refused when he asked her to mate with him and live with him in his dimension. Instead, she sent him away and raised her son who by the time I was ten was wearing dresses and already having my name changed." Cory grinned.

"Who fathered Jane and me?"

"Same man. We have the same parents, Ari. Vane came back yearly to see mom and me. He teased about us being his vacation. When I was nine, Mom found out she was pregnant again. Vane was thrilled, thinking he could convince her to finally come to his dimension. But, no, she refused.

"Jane was different. Not only was she born a girl," Cory said dryly, "but she was a practical child from the moment of her birth. Mom doted on her. She drove Vane nuts."

"Where is Vane now?" Ari almost did not want to know.

"In his dimension. With Mom."

"What? Is that where she went?" Ari gasped. "When she left us, I figured it was to go travelling like Ab-i-gail..." Her voice slowed on the last word. "Oh. I guess she did."

Snorting, Cory nodded. "Yeah, I never have understood why Destra wanted to make it sound as though she was dead. I asked her why she just didn't tell you and Jane the full truth, but she steadfastly refused." Her expression turned annoyed. "And look what it has done to you? If she had just been honest, none of this would have happened."

Shaking her head, Ari stared at the symbol on the floor. It all seemed crazy and even though she had been living it and wanted to consider it all a dream, she knew she hadn't. For one thing, she had a physical reminder, she thought as she caught a glimpse of her left ankle.

"When can I go home?" There didn't seem to be anything more Cory could tell her.

"Uh, Abigail said to wait until she got here. It seems the guy who took you really knows what he is doing. He's been involved with our family for a long time and this room is the only thing stopping him from taking you now."

"Great, just great," Ari sighed. A strange thought came to her. "How long was I over there?" She couldn't say "in his dimension" as weirdly enough that would make it too real.

"Three days. Oh, don't worry," she hastened on as Ari sat up straight in shock. "I called your work and told them you were deathly ill. Your boss said as soon as you felt better to call her."

"Feel better? I don't think that's ever going to happen."

For two days, Ari was rarely allowed to leave the tiny room. Whenever she had to use the bathroom, Cory practically had a panic attack and would stand outside and chant something the whole time she was in there. It was very hard to actually relax and use the facilities, Ari thought, when she was afraid someone was going to whisk her away to another dimension at any moment.

On day three, she woke up to find herself staring into the eyes of her grandmother. Her grandmother, who should look ancient, looked only a few years her senior. "Abigail," she said calmly, sitting up, not in the mood to hug the woman who seemed to have started the whole thing.

Abigail's lips twitched. "A bit angry with me, are

you? Well, I can't blame you there. Hard enough finding out you aren't even from this dimension, let alone being stolen away to another one without your okay."

After using the restroom, Ari walked back into the little room to find three chairs and a table had now taken up residence. The table had the same design as the floor. Both Cory and Abigail were seated, and breakfast was waiting for her.

For three days, she had been waiting impatiently for the arrival of her grandmother. Now suddenly she wished she would just go away. This was all her fault, after all. Sitting down with a huff, she dug into her pancakes with gusto.

The other two silently waited for her to finish, which just made her more aware they were there. Finally, when she cleaned the plate, Abigail began to speak. Her first words confused Ari. "Cory, please remove the plate and leave. What I have to say to Arwen is for her ears only."

"Good luck," her sister said with a wink, and then she was gone, closing the door behind her.

As her sister and the dishes were gone, she had nobody else to look at so she turned and looked into her grandmother's warm gray eyes. "Why?" There were so many questions she had, but the why was in everything. Why had he taken her? Why had she never been told? Why? Why? Why?

Nodding, Abigail leaned back. "As much as your mother refused to recognize the truth sitting in front of her at first, and Jane still refuses to even consider it, I think it is past time you learned who you are and where you came from. I will tell you everything. I know you will have a lot of questions. Please try to hold them back until I'm done."

Annoyed because Abigail sounded like a teacher speaking to her less-than-intelligent students, Ari gave her a sharp nod. *Get on with it, Abigail.*

Abigail's lips twitched in amusement before she began. "The first truth you must grasp is that this is not the only world there is. There are countless dimensions and realms. Some use the same spot in time and space and others do not. Most dimensions are filled with a conglomeration of beings, some good, some bad, all trying to make their way through their existence.

"Now, one of the ways this dimension differs from my own is the life expectancy. Earthlings only live sixty to eighty years unfortunately. My life expectancy is three to four thousand years." Ari's mouth dropped open. "As such, I have plenty of time to see what is truly out there. And that is the next truth you must learn to accept. Many other creatures know how to cross through the dimensional barrier. It is, as you have found, quite discombobulating at first as your body slowly shifts from one dimension to another. If you do it on purpose and shift intentionally, it is still uncomfortable, but it is less likely to make you ill."

Taking a drink from the glass of water in front of her, Abigail watched her granddaughter for a few minutes before continuing. "The third truth you must accept is that magic exists, though it is not what most earthlings think it is."

"Then what is it?" Ari asked, unable to stop herself.

"Most people here in this dimension seem to think magic is making something appear out of nowhere.

They insist magic is illogical and thus cannot exist." A slow chuckle left her lips. "Magic, Arwen Maria, is the ability to use energy to make things happen. Everyone and anyone has the ability to tap into this magic if they believe in it. Thankfully, the vast majority of people do not.

"There are, however"—Abigail's voice hardened— "three realms I know of where every being who resides there is intrinsically selfish and evil. A few of those individuals have embraced magic wholeheartedly."

"Orion."

She nodded her head. "Yes, Orion is from a realm so far away he never should have found you. If it hadn't been for the Interdimensional Dating Service, he would not have been able to." Anger seethed through her tone, and Ari wondered just how well the two knew one another. "He, unfortunately, is immortal. The bastard cannot die," she spat. "As I have no idea how long he has actually existed, I cannot tell you how long he has mastered the ability to use energy for his twisted desires, but it is at least five thousand years."

"Five thousand years!" Ari squeaked, unable even to think in those terms.

"Yes," Abigail said quietly, frowning. "Five thousand years ago, my great-aunt made a huge mistake. She was one of the first of our family to cross dimensions freely and did not know what to look out for. She crossed into his and was caught in his web. He used all his power to confuse and befuddle her until she was filled with fear and trepidation. She was the first of his slaves who held magical power. He thought he was one of the few who knew how to use it."

Her eyes turned cold as they locked on Ari's. "He

is smart, very smart. Never underestimate him, Arwen. After he learned about our family, he offered her a way out. He offered her a contract, which gave him access to certain women in our family who he could take at will once a century." Her voice turned colder. "Unfortunately, my great-aunt's line died out. So, for three centuries, he has not been able to take what he asserts is his. Finding you, I am sure he is salivating at the idea of making you his slave, Arwen."

Ari did not understand. This all sounded like some horror novel. "How did he know I was a relative?"

"Arwen, you are the spitting image of my great-aunt Celie. One look and he knew. And the moment he felt your presence enough in that coffee shop, well, he felt your energy signature, which is quite intense by the way, and could not wait to get you."

Could not wait to get you. Ari's throat closed up as her heart began to beat faster. "How can I defend myself against him?"

Abigail took a moment to answer, rubbing her thumbs up and down the glass she held. "Technically, you cannot."

Dread. Fear. She was doomed.

"At least not yet. But Cory and I discussed it when he took you, and I made a couple calls. The fact is, you need to be trained to block him and fight his control." She paused. "You wanted to accept it, didn't you?"

Ashamed, Ari nodded. "It seemed right."

"Of course it did. His power, combined with that horrible contract he and Celie drew up, created a very hard shield to get through."

"What is it about the contract and why is it still in force? Isn't there a judge who can nullify it?" Couldn't they just deny the contract?

"You have much to learn about magic, far more than Destra knew and even more than I know," Abigail answered, surprising her granddaughter. "You see, the contract was magically created between Orion and Celie while she was still under his power. The lawyers in this dimension are laughable when they say a contract is ironclad. They have no idea what that means."

Standing up, Abigail moved her arm and the table and chairs disappeared, leaving Ari and their glasses sitting suspended in air. "The contract they signed magically locks down to our very DNA." She made another movement and a long strand of DNA appeared, most of it white, with one strip of reddish orange wound around it. "You see the orange strand?"

"Yes."

"The contract is controlled by that particular strand. Anyone with that DNA has the possibility of being taken by Orion, and there is nobody who could, or even would, fight against it. The entire universe knows you cannot fight a magical contract. It is futile."

She walked up and grabbed the orange strand, unwrapping it from the rest. "Each one of these calls to him. If he decides to own that particular woman, all he has to do is ask her to accept his possession. Since her very own DNA is pulled to his ownership through the contract, she cannot nor does she wish to say no. The moment she says yes, this happens."

She tossed the strand back into the DNA where to Ari's horror, it seemed to take over. Slowly, each white piece began to turn, until a few minutes later, every piece was the same orange color. "It takes less than a second for this to happen."

"Oh my God," Ari gasped, wringing her hands together as the truth about what could have happened hit her. "I almost said yes."

"Why didn't you? No other woman in our family has been able to deny him."

"My ankle. It burned so badly, I shrieked 'no' instead."

Nodding, Abigail made another wave and the DNA disappeared, and the table and chairs reappeared.

Ari felt more comfortable knowing there was a chair holding her up. "Now, we will need to get you trained. I know of only two dimensions that are powerful enough magically that Orion dare not enter, Corofus and Zeta."

"Corofus?" Ari asked in surprise. "One of the guys who wrote me from IDS mentioned that. I thought it was a food."

Laughing, Abigail shook her head. "No, Corofus is a very strange place. Magical traders hang out there a lot, some of the best and worst of the galaxy. Orion used to hang out there, I'm told, until he screwed up too many deals. His eternal ban was the first of its kind. Zeta would probably fit your imagination a little more as to a magical world."

Zeta? Ari's eyes lit up. "My anklet was made there."

"Unfortunately, that is true. The Faerce Jewelry Makers have been around for many millennia. They make jewelry for many different reasons, each one imbued with a magical spell specifically created for its owner. About seven centuries ago, they entered into a contract with the Interdimensional Dating Service to provide magical talismans to their female clients to help them recognize men they might truly match well with. Obviously, yours was also able to tell you when evil contacted you."

Her head spun with all this new information, but if she had to go anywhere, Zeta sounded nicer than Corofus. "Why do you say unfortunately?"

A sad smile covered Abigail's face. "That mark on your ankle will be with you as long as you live. And whatever spell they cast upon that piece of jewelry will always be with you. That can be both a blessing and a curse, my dear. And as you have gone through the dimensional shift twice, and will soon go through it again, you will stop physically aging. You will remain with the body of a twenty-eight-year-old until you die."

Stunned, Ari stood up shakily and walked around the small room. "I won't age." Abigail shook her head. "Is that why you look to be in your thirties?"

Laughing, her grandmother nodded. "Yes, though I was technically one hundred and forty-two the first time I shifted dimensions. This is how one hundred forty-two looks in my dimension."

Looking her age for a long time did not sound like a bad thing, and she could go to this Zeta place and learn how to keep Orion at bay. Then it struck her. "I have to leave Earth permanently?" Her voice squeaked at the end. No more Cory? Or Jane? Or Denise?

Gently, Abigail stood up and walked over, placing an arm around her shoulders. "I know it sounds disheartening, Arwen, but there is a tremendous universe out there to be conquered. You can stay in contact with Cory and Jane.

"To make it seem as though you are still here, you

will need to keep up with the Interdimensional Dating Service though," she sighed. "Orion needs to think you are still leading a somewhat normal life."

"But if he thought he couldn't get me, wouldn't he just give up?" Ari asked hopefully, until she saw her grandmother's expression.

"No. Orion never gives up. Plus, if he thought you were suddenly unattainable, he might go after Cory or Jane just for spite. Since neither of them have a magical signature as strong as yours, it wouldn't be good."

Pain filled Abigail's eyes. "He would torture them until they were nothing but mindless broken bodies. And he would still come for you."

Depressed, but not one to just wallow, Ari took a deep breath and stood up straight. "Fine. So I guess I need to quit my job and pack up my belongings?"

"Cory is doing that now. She is grabbing the items that mean the most to you and dumping the rest. You will only be able to take a few things with you. And don't worry. You will not be going alone. I will accompany you to Zeta, since that seems to be your choice, and introduce you to Mayir, an old acquaintance of mine. He is strict and a bit of an asshole at times, to be honest, but if anyone can teach you how to deny Orion, it would be him."

A slightly evil glint came into her eyes, which made Ari wonder. "Why can't Orion visit Zeta?"

Abigail shook her head, her expression filled with sorrow. "Ask Mayir about it once you have been there for a while. You never piss off one of the fae folk. Never."

Chapter Eight - *Zeta*

As if things weren't going fast enough, Cory returned with three large suitcases comprising the only things in the world that Ari now owned. Two of them were filled with Abigail's gifts, the other contained her laptop, a few personal items, her address book, and a family picture.

"No clothes?" Ari asked confused, looking through all three cases. To be honest, she did not understand why Cory had retrieved all the Abigail gifts. Couldn't they have been left them behind in lieu of something to wear?

"No," Abigail answered shortly, quickly closing them all. "They have a specific kind of clothing on Zeta you will be expected to wear. The last thing you want to do is insult Mayir the first time you meet him." She grinned as another twinkle came into her eyes. "Leave that to zoors like Orion.

"Good choices," she added, nodding toward Ari's sister. "He needs to think she is here. As he has been to her apartment, he will look for her clothing when he cannot find her. I will drop these items in several different dimensions, lead him on a wild goose chase that should last at least a couple months. At some point, he will realize we have duped him, but by then, maybe Arwen will have enough power to resist him.

"This case has all you'll need," Abigail insisted,

pointing at the smallest of the suitcases with her laptop in it. "What did you tell her boss?" she asked, once again switching from talking to Ari to talking to her sister at lightning speed.

"That she died and we are having a private family ceremony," Cory replied simply.

A gasp left Ari's lips at the lie. "But I'm not dead!"

"You will not be coming back, Arwen," her grandmother scolded. "And even if you could stay, you would never age. It wouldn't be as though you could keep that job anyway. Now, come. Grab your bag and let's go."

Cory pulled her into a bone-crushing hug. "Keep in touch," she whispered. "And contact Mom. I bet she and Vane would love to come say hi."

Ari nodded and, as Cory stepped back, she picked up her smallest suitcase. She watched her sister walk out of the room and close the door, and she realized she had never felt so alone. She would almost be willing to go back and be on a date with Jay. Almost. A giggle left her lips. Nothing was that bad.

Abigail grabbed her left hand and pulled her into the center of the room over the insignia. As she began to chant nonsense words and grunts, Ari clutched her suitcase to her. The now familiar feeling of having the world she was in fade while something else took its place made her shudder. With any luck, Orion would accidentally shift into the sun, burn up, and she could go back to her regular life. If only she could figure out how to look as though she was growing older, and of course, there would be the pesky explanation of how she'd returned from the dead.

The walls receded and in their place, muted greens,

browns, and blues began to appear. She stared at them, feeling fuzzy, as though her eyesight was out of focus. Abigail's chanting grew louder and the air around them grew colder. The green began to take form, looking like tall thick grass, waving in the wind. The blues intensified into crystalline blue flowers. The brown came into focus as tree trunks, a dirt path, and then so did other colors and hues begin to take shape.

Blinking her eyes, Ari realized she and Abigail stood in the middle of an unpaved road with grass, taller than they were, on each side. Each stem was about four inches thick and, about three feet up on each blade of grass, lay a beautiful flower with four light blue petals that looked like crystal surrounding a dark blue center. Above them was the sky, but it wasn't a sky Ari was at all familiar with. It was pale lavender. "Wow."

A snort came from her grandmother. "Well, we are here, but not in the right place. Come, we need to find a clothing merchant and then Mayir." Abigail set a very fast pace, forcing Ari to hurry in order to keep up. It was a good thing she was into running, or she might have been left behind. For over an hour, they followed the very straight path through the tall grass, not coming across anywhere or anyone, and Ari was beginning to feel light-headed. A childish desire to ask "Are we there yet?" came to her, but she did not voice it.

Pet. His soft voice infiltrated her mind and she gasped, going still as stone.

"Arwen, we cannot dawdle!"

Pet, I will find you. Return and your punishment will not be as bad as it could be. Return, pet. NOW!

A cry left her lips as her body of its own accord

seemed to want to follow his voice.

"Arwen!" Abigail snapped, shaking her. "What is going on?"

"He's calling to me," she said through frozen lips. "He wants me to return to him."

"He's already found you!" Abigail screamed, releasing her granddaughter. "There is only one way that could have happened. He is following me." She took three steps backward and began to make some strange hand movements. "Follow this road. Tell the first individual you come to, the following: 'I am a gift from Abigail of Corlanos for Mayir. Please deliver me quickly.'"

"What!" screeched Ari as the words and the realization her grandmother was leaving her combined. "A gift?"

"Just say it, Arwen! Mayir knows you are coming, and it will keep you safe. He will just have to accept that he will have to get you your uniform. Say it!"

Pet! Return now.

Whimpering, Ari whispered, "I am a gift from Abigail of Corlanos for Mayir. Please deliver me quickly."

As soon as the words left her lips, Abigail disappeared and so did Orion's voice.

"I hope this is a dream and I will wake up soon," she whispered, grasping her suitcase tighter and continuing along the road. As the lavender above began to deepen to a purple, she wondered if she would have to spend the night where she was. But even with the dark purple, she could still see the road ahead so she kept walking.

And walking.

And walking.

With each step she took, she repeated the words to herself that Abigail had told her to speak, hoping if she messed it up, they would get the gist of it, whoever they were. And that brought up the question, who were they? Were they like her? Or would they be more like him? Shivering at the thought of the man with cold red eyes, she began to whistle as she walked.

It was a strange road, never ending, never turning and never getting anywhere. As the purple began to lighten to lavender and her gaze turned a little hazy due to exhaustion, she began to wonder if she would ever find anyone, or if she was doomed to walk this path forever.

The first time she heard *it*, she paused and cocked her head. Murmurs. Definite murmurs. People! Quickening her step, she had a renewed sense of something. She couldn't call it hope, because she was worried about what she would find, but it was nice to know she would soon run into one of the citizens of Zeta. The knowledge that she was dressed in a pair of her sister's pajamas did not daunt her step. She was tired and hungry. Surely, these people would be friendly. They made her that anklet, and it was the most beautiful thing she had ever seen. In fact, before she left, she might see if she could get a few more pieces. Though hopefully these wouldn't melt into her skin.

Strange sounds of *poof, poof, poof*, filled the air, and she slowed down as they became louder. To her surprise, the blue flowers ceased to exist about five feet in front of her. The grass was still there, but not a flower in sight. The flowers next to her began to disappear, each one making the *poof* noise as they left.

No longer hearing the murmurs, but a little afraid to stay in a spot where things were disappearing, she forced her legs to speed up.

The grass disappeared on her left. *POOF!* On her right. *POOF!*

A scream left her lips as she hit the ground, afraid that whatever was taking the grass would take her too.

"Vast!" hollered a voice that was echoed all around by other voices.

A moment later, a shadow loomed over her. Oh, no. Please let them not be angry with her. "Va misra loe?" A long thin white hand appeared in front of her. Figuring the person was offering her a hand up, she gingerly took it and stood up. Looking up, her eyes fell on the man who had helped her to her feet. Unable to judge age by looks anymore, she noted he had long brown hair and bright blue eyes the color of the flower petals. His face was long and angular and he wore a nice smile. "Corlya loe?"

Having no idea what he was saying, she opened her mouth to say so when she remembered what her grandmother said to say. Clearing her throat, she said, "I am a gift from Abigail of Corlanos for Mayir. Please deliver me quickly."

His eyes widened, even as his smile dimmed. Then he nodded. "Of course," he said in a soft voice. "I apologize for scaring you. Clearing the Molara fields can be a tedious job, and sometimes we forget travelers take this road. Come. I will take you to Mayir." He turned and shouted a few more words that made no sense to her and then turned back to her. It just occurred to her that her hand was still in his when the world she was looking at disappeared and in its place was a tall

117

white wall made of stone. Turning around she saw they stood in front of a large building. Behind them were fields and fields of flowers without another building in sight. "I hope Mayir is everything you were promised," he said, leaning down to kiss her hand. "If he bothers you, please call out for Verisha and I will come."

He dropped her hand, banged on the wall, and then quickly disappeared. Zeta was an odd place. The next time she saw Abigail she would let her know what she thought of being dumped here. A squeak left her lips as a door opened in the stone wall, and a tall man with cold blue eyes surveyed her. "Va misra loe?" he asked in a much colder voice than Verisha. His whole persona told her to go away, but she wasn't about to stop now.

Taking a deep breath, she said in a loud voice, "I am a gift from Abigail of Corlanos for Mayir. Please deliver me quickly."

His cold eyes seemed to become even colder, but he stood back and held the door open, so she went inside.

She had been wrong. The stone was not the wall of a building, it was the wall of a fortress. Inside the wall was a large garden separated into sections. Grass with blue flowers like she had seen before. Grass with purple flowers, green flowers, pink flowers, opaque flowers…everywhere she looked was a different section of flowers separated by a stone walkway. But the scary thing was that lining the inside of the wall were men, lots of lots of men, who were dressed like warriors. They even had swords.

What did a magical people need with swords?

"You would keep Mayir waiting?" he asked in a haughty voice, and she looked up to realize he was several feet away. Quickly, she followed him.

The garden seemed to go on forever, just like the wall of soldiers did. Finally, they came to a set of steps that rose to a doorway. She hoped Mayir was in there. He took three steps at a time and she was so tired that taking them one by one seemed a chore. By the time she got to the top, she was breathing hard, and he gave her a disdainful glare before opening the door to usher her inside.

Inside, the walls were of the same stone as the fortress, and while she could not tell where the light was coming from, the hallway they walked down was well lit. At the end, he opened a set of doors and walked in, shouting something at the top of his lungs. Cautiously she followed him.

The room was large, square, and made from the same stone. Light and open, it had three pieces of furniture. A large chair, a small table beside it, and a small footstool. On the chair sat the most interesting man she had ever seen. Thin and wiry with a gaunt face, pointy ears, long white hair, and bushy eyebrows, he made her think of a Santa who must have lost weight really fast. He turned and nodded at the man who had shown her in and he left quickly.

"So, you are Abigail's granddaughter," he said in a smooth, deep voice. "Come." He pointed at a spot a few feet in front of him, and she quickly walked over to it. His eyes took in everything, her face, hair, clothing and from the frown on his face, she was sure he would throw her out. Instead, he chuckled. Surprisingly, it did not lighten his face. It made him look ill. "She was right. Your magical signature is extreme—almost as powerful as mine. She should have sent you to me for training years ago, but never mind. Training starts tomorrow."

He stood up and walked to the wall behind his chair. "Come. You need a change of clothing, food, and sleep. I'm surprised you have not passed out." He opened a door she had not even realized was there and quickly began to ascend a set of stone steps. As she followed him, she began to think everything here was made with that white stone.

They climbed two sets of stairs ending at a doorway. He opened it and as she walked inside, she gasped. The bedroom was decorated in whites and lavenders. It had a bed in the middle, a side table, and a dresser. "Strip all your clothing off and toss it in that basket," he said pointing to a simple stone garbage pail. He didn't even move and a tray of food appeared on the side table. "Eat as much as you can and then get into bed. You will sleep until I believe you are ready." Without another word, he turned and left.

"Well, isn't he bossy," she muttered as she began to take her clothing off. Once she was in the buff, she tossed it at the pail, gasping as it disappeared the moment it hit. "Oh great. Now I have nothing to wear."

The scent of the food pulled at her as well as the bed, but her stomach won out.

None of the food on the tray looked familiar, but it all smelled so good she ate quickly. The scents, the flavors, and the textures combined to make the most amazing meal she had ever eaten. "His chef should open up a restaurant in the United States," she giggled as she licked the plate clean. "He or she would make a killing."

As soon as she ate the food and drank the tall glass

of water, which was the best she had ever tasted in her entire life, she crawled under the covers and moaned. The bed was comfortable too.

Maybe I'll just stay here forever...

Chapter Nine - *Magic, not all it's cracked up to be*

Stretching, Ari sighed. She was so comfortable she didn't want to wake up. Something told her she should open her eyes. Pulling one lid open, she shrieked as she spotted Mayir at the foot of her bed. "What are you doing?" she snapped, annoyed.

He raised an eyebrow. "You have fifteen minutes to eat and dress. Then we start your training." Without another word, he disappeared.

Mayir. Zeta. That's right. She was clear cross the universe on a distant planet with some guy who was supposed to teach her magic. Flumping back on her pillows, she stared up at the stone ceiling. Sleeping the day away did not seem like such a bad idea, especially after her recent brush with Orion the terrifying.

"If you are not dressed, you will still appear at my side. I suggest you move."

Gasping, she sat up and looked around, grimacing as she realized he was able to speak to her without being in the room, just like Orion. That was just a tad annoying and a whole lot scary. Getting out of bed, she quickly ate the breakfast that was waiting for her, another meal to tempt anyone's taste buds, and looked around for what to wear.

At first, she refused to believe that the strange diaphanous material hanging from the doorway was her outfit. It couldn't be. It was so girly. "Ewww," she groaned as she pulled it down. It looked like some crazy outfit a Disney princess might wear. In three pieces, her uniform consisted of a pale yellow skirt that was in about fifty layers, a deep blue bustier, and a white lace camisole to wear under it.

After laying each piece out on the bed, she realized there was something missing. "Uh, Mayir?" she said, feeling stupid for talking into thin air. "Where's the underwear?"

"The what?"

"Underwear. You know. To wear underneath the frilly skirt."

There was a moment of silence and then he said, *"Ah, you mean this?"* A pair of granny panties in the same material as the camisole appeared.

"Yeah, that will do. If it must," she added in an undertone.

"If you dislike my choices in clothing, maybe you will learn magic faster so as to create your own."

Rolling her eyes, she put on the panties and cami before glaring at the skirt. She shimmied into it, trying not to laugh at how stupid she felt, before grabbing the bustier. It was more of a chore. It had laces she had to pull tight, so as not to show everything off. As it was, when she got it tied tightly enough, her breasts puffed out the top. A mirror stood near the door. She walked over and looked at it. "I look like a naughty cupcake."

Her legs were viewable, even under the layers and layers of transparent fabric. The bustier pushed her breasts up until they were about to overflow. Colors of the gown reminded her of a cartoon she saw when she was a kid. "I'm Snow White in an R-rated flick." Giggling, she barely began to turn toward the door when her room disappeared, and she found herself outside. Underneath her feet was soft dirt, and as she turned around she realized that was all she could see. No buildings, no flowers, no grass. Nothing but dirt and lavender sky. Well, at least she was still on Zeta.

"This is your first lesson," said Mayir's disembodied voice. *"You are to bring grass into life where there is none."*

After a few minutes of nothing, she asked, "And just how am I supposed to do that?"

"Magic."

Rolling her eyes, she glared into the dirt. "Did Abigail not inform you I know nothing of magic?"

"That matters not. You will bring it to life because you can. When you have finished, you will come back."

"You have got to be kidding me!" she spat. "I know Abigail muttered nonsense words to get us here. Surely there are—"

"Enough wasting time," he said in a firm voice. *"Magic is simple, Arwen Reynolds. Think it. Believe it. Understand. Let it happen. That is all you need. Now, I am busy. Do not bother me."*

Gasping, she opened her mouth to let him have it when she remembered Abigail saying something about what a pain in the ass he was. "Great. A beastly red-eyed dude wants me as his slave, and instead I end up taking lessons from Professor I-Have-My-Head-Up-My-Ass. If I was home, this would be Jane's idea of a date."

Huffing, she looked around.

Dirt, dirt, dirt, as far as the eye could see. He wanted her to bring grass into the world. That made no sense. For hours, she walked around in circles trying to figure out how to get grass to grow. She tried to command it. "Grass grow!" But all she got was a deep chuckle that resounded in her head. Mayir obviously thought that was funny.

She dug into the dirt looking for any sign of life. None found. For over an hour, she sat on the dirt and tried to imagine the vista in front of her covered in green. Nothing happened. As the sun reached its height and began to go down again, she was so bored she stood up and began to dance, figuring maybe she could get some rain to come and it would make the grass grow.

By the time the sun went down, she was tired, grumpy, hungry, and trying to decide who she would kill first: Orion, Abigail, or Mayir?

"Hungry?"

"Very." A table, chair, and full meal appeared before her, and without thinking, she sat down and dug into it. Every time she drained her glass of water, it refilled itself. Entranced, she tossed out the fourth glass and waited for it to refill, but it did not. Grimacing, she finished her meal and looked around. "Now what?"

"Make the grass appear."

"But I don't know how," she whined.

"Start there. For it is at the unknowing where magic begins."

Well that made a whole lot of sense.

Frowning, she stood up and walked around in the moonlight, unsurprised when she turned around and the table and chair were gone.

She was surprised however, to find a bed in its place.

"Sleep and try again tomorrow."

"I'm sleeping outside?"

When he did not respond, she sighed and walked to the bed. Too tired to care that she was dressed and covered in dirt, she climbed in and pulled the blanket up to her chin. As soon as her head hit the pillow, she fell asleep. For days, she woke up in the field, tried to figure out how to get grass to appear, did not succeed, and fell asleep in the field. After a full week, she was tired of it all.

"Look!" she said loudly as once again a table, chair and food appeared. "I told you, but you obviously did not believe me. I can't do this!"

A deep chuckle rang through her head. *"Can you not?"* He appeared right in front of her. "Tell me why you cannot."

"Because I don't know how." Duh.

"Do you know what grass looks like?"

"Well, of course, but—"

"Can you imagine the field covered in it?"

"Well, sure, but—"

"Close your eyes."

"Why?"

He raised an eyebrow, and with a huff she closed her eyes. "See the field in your mind." Grumbling under her breath, she focused on the dirt and imagined it covered in spiky green grass. "Feel it beneath your feet." She dug her toes into the dirt, trying to imagine it was spiky winter grass instead. "Now, let it go."

Her eyes opened. "What do you mean?"

"First you imagine. Then you feel. Then you understand. Once you understand, you can let it go and it will happen."

Frowning, she glared at the dirt. "I can't do it."

"Could you imagine it?"

"Yes."

"Could you feel it?"

"Sort of."

"Could you understand?"

"What am I supposed to understand?"

To her annoyance, he nodded. "That is where your block is. Understanding." She opened her mouth to ask what he meant when he turned to the wide expanse of dirt. "First imagine." His eyes glazed over. "Then you feel it." His fingers twitched and his toes dug into the dirt. "Then you understand." A look of peace crossed his face. "Then you let it go." As the words left his lips, the entire field went from being one large dirt pile to a huge green field.

"How did you do that?" she whispered, reaching down and pulling up a blade of it. "And more importantly, why couldn't I?"

"I explained how I did it, Arwen. As for why you did not, it is because you do not understand yourself. Come, let us return. You need to contact the Interdimensional Dating Service so that Orion still thinks you are available."

Confused, she nodded, and next thing she knew, she was in her bedroom with a full meal in front of her and her laptop booted up right next to it. Electing to eat first, she slowly ate the food, her mind trying to make sense of the last few days.

"What did you learn today?" His voice made her jump, and she turned and glared at him.

She was tired and achy and just wanted things to go back to normal. "That there must be something wrong with me, because I couldn't get it to work!"

"Very good, Arwen. First lesson learned." As he disappeared, she gaped at where he was.

"Abigail, come rescue me," she sighed, finishing her dinner.

Chapter Ten - *Contact*

Once her dinner was done and the plates disappeared, she turned to her laptop.

It felt strange pulling up her email address. How did it even connect with the internet on Earth? Having been away from Earth for at least a week, she wondered how many emails would appear. Never would she have expected only fifteen emails. All of them from IDS. "I guess the other two services have forgotten me," she said in amusement.

"Actually, Abigail discontinued your use of them as they were not involved."

"I wish you would stop talking in my head," she murmured. "It is too much like him."

"You might as well get used to it," he said from right behind her.

Rolling her eyes, she pulled up the IDS folder. Of the fifteen messages, twelve of them were from Orion. Two were from names she did not recognize and one was from Terrian.

"Open up the messages from Orion."

She opened up the oldest one.

Come back now, pet.
Orion

A small twinge came in her chest, and she rubbed it frantically.

"Unfortunately you will probably feel that for a

long time. Orion knew what he was doing when he created that contract and with Celie doing her best to please him, she just made it worse. In his mind, he was after her family, essentially all female descendants. Instead, she gave him access to every female member of her blood line. And he really wants you," he growled.

"But why? I mean, Abigail said I look like her great aunt, but I still don't understand why he would focus so much on me. I'm really not all that special."

When he didn't respond, she looked over her shoulder. He was looking at her with the strangest expression. "Have you no idea of your worth?"

Blushing a little, she shrugged. "I'm not downing myself, but this is huge. Why me?"

"Because your magical signature is more intense than any woman in your family. Ever. Because you carry with you the magic held within only one other being." When she raised her eyebrow, he continued. "Your grandfather. His power is phenomenal. And Orion wants it." Before she could ask, he disappeared.

"Who's my grandfather?"

He didn't answer.

Frustrated, but knowing he would not give up the information until he was ready, she turned back to her laptop. Wanting to get all of Orion's messages out of the way, she went through them quickly.

> *Where are you, pet?*
> *Respond or there will be consequences.*
> *Where has Abigail taken you?*
> *Answer me!*

Each message became more demanding, his anger practically ripping through them. By the time the final one appeared, her chest ached, and she whimpered aloud as she read it.

You are mine. I own you. Either come to me or the pain will get worse every day. I might not even accept you back if you wait too long. Think of it, pet. A lifetime of anguish.

Her hands shook as she hit reply. Her mind thought about what she wanted to say. Stay away from me, go away, and I am not your slave were what she thought. What she typed was *Yes, Master.* As soon as she saw the words, she let out a scream and erased them.

Concentrate, Arwen.

Concentrate. Great advice! Maybe when she figured out magic she could turn him into a toad.

Looking at the last message, her finger paused over the delete button, but a thrum in her ankle made her pause. She was prepared to think Terrian was some lunatic with his description, but the fact was, he was probably real. A man from a different dimension. Even though she was sitting on Zeta, it still felt unreal. What was it Abigail said? Something about the anklet having the ability to help her find a good match? Well, it certainly didn't hate Terrian like it did Orion, which was a huge plus. She really needed to ask about what was done to the metal to make her ankle do this. Deciding she would give him another chance, she opened his email.

Arwen,

Was I too forward in my previous email? If so, I apologize. I have been told I can act too bold at times.

I hope you are well and that whether or not you respond that you are happy.

Terrian

The email was nice and made her feel good, just like his first one did. Reminding herself there were, in fact, other dimensions and she needed to remember that, she opened up the email he wrote that freaked her out and reread it.

Arwen,

That is a beautiful name. So, you live in a library as well? Well, that is wonderful to hear. Though maybe not for you. It can be a bit taxing. I thought it would be nice to tell you a little more about myself, if that would be acceptable to you. If not, read no further.

I am a rather large sports enthusiast and wish I could spend more time engaged in them rather than watching. My favorites are wind surfing and tree skiffing. Do not spread this around, but I also have a deep love for animals. My mount Abriethon has been with me for a few decades, and I swear he knows me more than anyone else. I also raise Dipthan Kivees, somewhat similar to the Orenean Brevs, but my mother and I have been striving to breed the perfect corg with a more malleable temper.

Have you ever jumped dimensions before? I did when I was much younger. Unfortunately I found it did not bode well for my temperament so I stopped. My brothers Caifu and Stero spent a couple centuries doing it and it never affected them, though, so it might just be me. My youngest brother Zenun jumped once but found the shift too painful. He stayed in the Anjolan Sphere for fifty years before he was killed accidentally. We tried to get him to come back home before then, but he stubbornly refused.

I was sorry to hear you lost your mother. Losing one's parent must be a dreadful experience. My mother has just passed her millennial birthday and is stronger than ever. My father is close to his bimillenial. I am quite young at only 745 years. Within my direct family, I have two older brothers and seven younger. There are many other relations who I will not mention as to do so would take far too much space.

Besides the books I have read, I am unfamiliar with your particular dimension. Would you be willing to tell me about it? Or anything you wish to write about. I would just like to get to know you better.

Looking forward to your next message,
Terrian

Suddenly the whole email made a lot more sense. And it made him look more normal, if normal was having a conversation with someone from a different dimension. Feeling, hoping actually, that maybe he was someone she could talk to, just like she thought, she hit reply.

Terrian,

I apologize for not responding earlier. My life has taken an unexpected turn. You might be surprised to find out that a week ago I had no idea there were actual dimensions or that other worlds existed. I thought the

Interdimensional Dating Service was on Earth. So, when I read your second email I am afraid I thought you were a lunatic.

Sorry about that.

The fact is, of all the guys who showed interest from IDS and the two earth-bound services I tried, you seemed the most human. Ha. That sounds funny now.

So, do you mind if I ask some questions?

What is tree skiffing? What are Dipthan Kivees, Orenean Brevs, and what is a corg?

I'm sorry to hear your younger brother died in another dimension, but I must admit I'm still trying to wrap my head around the whole thing. And not just the dimensions, but the age thing. Humans live somewhere around 70 years. You have lived 10x that much. I cannot even fathom the things you have seen in your 745 years. Makes my 28 seem like nothing.

Oh, and my mother isn't dead. She left us ten years ago. I thought it was to tour the globe like I thought my grandmother was doing. Uhh, nope. Turns out my mother skipped to another dimension to live with the man who fathered me and both of my sisters. All I know about him is his name is Vane. And my grandmother? She looks 33 and is actually several centuries old.

And now she tells me, I won't age because I have now jumped dimensions a few times. Not voluntarily, but I guess it doesn't matter.

Ever feel as though life is going faster

than you planned?
  So, what dimension are you from?
  Arwen

She reread her note and it sounded convoluted and strange, but then that was how she felt. Given Abigail and Mayir's instructions, she knew she couldn't tell him where she was just in case Orion was able to intercept her communication. It made it hard to build anything, even a friendship, when you could not tell the entire truth.

Chapter Eleven - *So Much Worse Than Doomed*

"What do you know?" Mayir asked as she stood in front of him in his stone room.

She glared at him. She had now been on Zeta for two weeks, and as far as she could tell, she had learned nothing. "What do I know? You send me out into that dirt on a daily basis, telling me to make grass appear, and yet you don't tell me how to do it. I'm left out there with no instructions for a week before you bring me back. Why don't you just tell me how to do it?" she asked desperately. Staring at dirt day-in, day-out was beginning to make her feel loopy.

Sighing, he shook his head. "Do you remember what I told you about how magic is accomplished?"

Barely able to stop herself from rolling her eyes, she nodded. Just five days ago, he reprimanded her for doing it. Made her feel about two feet tall. "Yes. First imagine. Then you feel it. Then you understand. Then you let it go. I get the first two parts, but I don't understand what I am supposed to understand."

Placing his hands together with each of his fingertips meeting while the palms stayed as far away as possible, he surveyed her. "I see," he said simply, standing up. With a wave of his hand a table appeared to her right and she turned and looked at it, half expecting food as that was what usually appeared when she was frustrated. Instead, the table had a plate and a glass, but nothing was in or on them.

"We do not do magic, Arwen. Ever. It is the universe and the energy that abounds that does it. All we are is a conduit. Come." He walked over to the table and she followed. "What are you hungry for?"

It sounded like a simple enough question, though she had come to understand there were no simple questions from him. Every question had a deeper meaning.

"I don't know any of the names of the food I've eaten here."

"Doesn't matter. What are you in the mood for? Don't tell me. Imagine it. Close your eyes and see the food in your head."

Closing her eyes, a vision of a piece of molten chocolate cake came to mind. In the center was gooey fudge that seeped out of the sides of the cake, and on top were swirls of rum icing. Her tongue slid along her lower lip just thinking about it, the way the chocolate slid across her tongue, bringing out all the wonderful flavors, and how the icing would stick to her top lip. She could practically smell it.

"Who can give you what you desire?"

"It comes from a restaurant just a few mi-"

He interrupted her. "No. Do not think logically, Arwen. Magic is the antithesis of logic. Who can give you what you desire?"

Frowning, she concentrated on the memory of the cake as it slid down her throat. Who could give it to her? Mayir seemed to think magic could, and he was able to make all sorts of strange things appear out of nowhere. "You can," she responded.

"True, but I do not know what it is that is giving

you that look of pure pleasure. Only you know. So, again I ask, who can give you what you desire?"

She knew what he was asking, and yet she wasn't sure she could do it. "I know you are trying to get me to say I can, but I don't know if I can."

"All right. Go through the steps in your mind again. Let your desire fill you with each step."

Taking a deep breath, she nodded and imagined the cake sitting on that white plate all gooey and delicious. Her logical mind wanted to rush through it, but she refused and just sat there until the only thing in her mind was the cake. Then she went on to the next step. Her hand tingled as she could feel herself picking up a fork, dipping it into the deep chocolaty goodness, and putting it in her mouth. The texture, taste, and scent hit her and she moaned. Knowing she needed to go even though she wanted to stay right there in that step, she moved on to Understanding.

What was she to understand? That she was able to do magic, though that still seemed far-fetched. That magic was not logical and as such, maybe it couldn't be pinned down. Her head cocked to the side as she considered that. Her mind wanted to pin it down, to discover each step perfectly so that it could be done the same way each time. But what if that was the wrong way to go about it? What if instead of knowing, it was in the unknowing where magic began? What if instead of knowing the steps, all she had to know was the end result? A soft gasp left her lips at the possibilities.

"Good. Now, let it go, Arwen. Let go of the need to control. Let go of the desire to accomplish. Let go of your version of reality. Accept the universe and energy will make what you have decided upon appear. Just let it go."

Shivering, which surprised her, she forced herself to relax while mentally telling herself it was the end result that matters. *How it gets there is not my job.*

A low chuckle rumbled in front of her. "Open your eyes, Arwen."

Blinking, she looked at him. He wore a smug expression, and when she raised an eyebrow, he nodded toward the plate. Her knees buckled as she turned her head, and what she saw sitting on that beautiful white plate was exactly what she had imagined. Even the fudge was dribbling out of a small hole on the side. "Wow."

"Eat. Ruminate. After you eat, go check your messages and then go to bed. Tomorrow is a busy day." Without another word, he disappeared, or to be more exact she and the food disappeared and reappeared in her room.

The cake was everything she remembered and imagined, and she took her time eating it and licking the plate clean. Thankfully, the glass kept filling with water because she was thirsty. She hoped he would send her back to the dirt the next day. She was ready to make the grass grow.

As soon as there wasn't even a scrap left on the plate, she turned to her laptop. It had now been a week since she wrote Terrian. Would he have responded? Or blown her off? She was sure there would be responses from Orion, but she had already decided to delete them without looking.

There were, in fact, seven messages from *AttractivelyAgile*. One even had a paperclip. As her chest tightened and her ankle sizzled, she quickly deleted them all. She was happy she was learning, because she really needed to be able to fight off his control. Freaky, red-eyed, demon weirdo.

The last message was from Terrian and with a little hope and excitement, she opened it.

Arwen,

First off, let me say I was pleased to receive your message. If I might ask, how did you join the Interdimensional Dating Service if you were unaware of different dimensions? I have turned the matter over to one of our security people to see if IDS has done something they shouldn't. For it is against their charter to advertise in dimensions that are not advanced.

It must have been a shock to learn about the polarity of time and space. It took me three centuries to finally understand it, and I grew up with it.

Which dimension is your mother in? I was pleased she is still alive, especially as now you can get into contact with her much easier.

As for the animals I mentioned, yes, you must have wondered if I was some deranged vrill trying to mess with you. I am unsure how to explain them as I do not know what animals in your dimension look like. I have attached a couple of images of two of my favorite corgs, so you can see what Dipthan Kivees are. There are several different breeds of corgs. Dips, as we call them, are just one.

As for tree skiffing, we have a motorized board we use to jump along the tops of the

*trees. It is exceptionally exciting to do it on top
of a mountain, to feel all that fresh air while
knowing if you slip it is a long way down.
Considering how my brother's wives feel
about it, I can assume you are grimacing right
now. I assure you, it is fun.*

*I would love to hear more about Earth
and what you enjoy doing when you are not in
the library. Do you have a job? Travel? What
are your favorite foods?*

*As I mentioned before, I am usually too
busy to do something fun, but one of the things
I do enjoy is riding. I have attached an image
of Abriethon, my mount. I got him fifty-seven
years ago. He has a good twelve to fifteen left
in him. Once a week, I take him out of our
hamlet and ride. It is very freeing. Do you
have a similar animal there?*

*Well, I will leave you be for now. Thank
you so much for writing and explaining what
was going on. I appreciate your honesty.*

Until your next letter,
Terrian

Grinning like a stupid little girl with her first crush,
Ari read the message three times before responding.
Bringing up the attached photos, she relaxed. Corgs
were dogs. His kind of looked like a Doberman
pinscher/poodle cross. Abriethon looked similar to a
horse, well a caricature of a horse anyway, with his
large haunches and thin legs.

As she replied, she told him as much as she felt she
could, which wasn't much, about her current situation.
She did fill him in on what was wonderful about

Tucson, Arizona, from the dust storms and the monsoons to the cactus, the mountains, and the wonderful dry heat. By the end of her message, she had described all about her best friend's warty pig obsession, her love of running in the park, and about her sisters and her nieces and nephews. In the end, she left him with the truth.

It is great to converse with someone who understands about the dimensions. There is still so much for me to learn and I feel like I am running out of time. I am only allowed on the internet every once in a while as someone found me on IDS, and he is not a good individual. I hope, once this is all over, I can get to know you more.

To happier days,

Arwen

The next four days were brutal. Mayir did not send her out to make grass. "You have learned that lesson. Now you must use what you have learned to defend yourself." The term defend was confusing until he had one of the sullen-faced guards come in. Her first thought was she would need to learn to defend herself physically and she was doomed. But as the guard turned to look at her, she felt a great whoosh of energy hit her chest, and she fell backward, stopping an inch from the floor.

She had to learn to defend herself against magic. So much worse than doomed.

Every day, she was attacked magically with no way to defend herself. Tossed around the room like a rubber ball, the only good thing was that Mayir did not allow her to be harmed. When magic would thrust her into a wall, she would stop an inch or two from it.

So although she had no concussions at least, her entire body ached from the force of the magic used against her.

"Defend yourself," one of his goons said walking up to her at the end of the fifth day. She was exhausted, angry, and just wanted them all to go away. Since the chocolate cake incident, she had magicked all her food and had become quite adept at it. Her clothing, however still wasn't up to par. Ignoring that, she quickly went through the steps.

Imagine: She saw the goon as a fly and in her hand was a fly swatter.

Feel: She felt the joy as her hand swung the swatter and squished him against the wall.

Understand: She knew that the end result, squashed fly, was all that mattered, the rest was up to the universe.

Let it go: Mentally, she let control go and thanked the universe for making the end result happen.

And then she opened her eyes.

His brown eyes stared into hers with an amused expression. Looking at her hand, she was embarrassed to see it holding a fly swatter and it was resting against the back of his head.

"You thought you could hit me with that? What is it supposed to do?" he asked before bursting into laughter. Mayir's laughter joined his and before long, several other goons walked in and burst out laughing as well.

Embarrassed, she ran through the steps in her head and quickly appeared in her bedroom, sans laughing men. Since it wasn't dinner time yet, and she had some time to kill because she wasn't about to embarrass herself again, she turned on her laptop.

"You may hide for the rest of the day. Tomorrow you will learn how to defend yourself."

Muttering under her breath about obnoxious know-it-alls, she turned a little pink when his rumbling laughter filled her head.

She would seriously let Abigail have it the next time she saw her for sticking Ari with Mayir. It seemed to her he enjoyed torturing her over and over again before finally teaching her what she needed to know.

Pulling up her email, she waited as seven messages downloaded, surprised when the screen blipped three times like it had back on earth.

"Mayir?" she called.

"Yes?"

"My computer blipped like it did back on earth. Should I be worried?" Like about Orion finding me, she thought, staring at the IDS folder.

"Even if he found you here, he couldn't do anything about it. Delete his emails and move on to the one you want to read." The amusement in his voice just made her more annoyed. How did he know she was looking forward to Terrian's email? *"And by the way, Arwen, Terrian of the Delania Dimension is a great catch. Females throughout the dimensions have been trying to catch him for centuries. Well done."*

"Wait...but..." she spluttered, embarrassed. "I haven't caught him. We're just talking."

"Of course you are. Say yes to what he asks."

Shaking her head and electing to not say anything else—he would probably just tease her more—she quickly deleted Orion's messages, once again hit with pain in her chest as she did so. Rubbing it, she opened Terrian's message.

Arwen,

> *It sounds like you are under a tremendous amount of stress right now. Finding out you are not from your own planet, that other dimensions exist, and that someone from a different dimension is after you. That is a century worth of stress, or at least it sounds that way to me.*

> *Can you give me the name, or at least the username, of the individual who is after you? My security force is in contact with IDS and have complete freedom to jump to any dimension they want to, though not the realms, unfortunately. They are too dangerous for even our security forces to enter.*

> *I do wish to help you, if you would let me,*

> *Terrian*

As her ankle tingled and a nice warm feeling seemed to invade her, completely dissolving the tightness in her chest, Ari sat back. He sounded so wonderful, but then again, she hadn't met him yet. "You know Terrian?" she asked.

"I met him once and know his parents quite well." His voice from directly behind her no longer startled her. She was too used to him popping up unexpectedly.

"He is asking for Orion's name. Says he wants to help. But Orion is from one of the realms, so I doubt it would make a difference."

"It would make a great difference," he disagreed. "Arwen, what have you learned about magic so far?" Instead of commanding, for the first time he actually sounded interested in her answer. As such, she wasn't as flippant as she would normally be.

"It's there and I can't control the magic itself. Just the end result. And even that I can't control against a more formidable opponent," she sighed, thinking of the fly swatter incident as she turned in her chair to face him.

"Do you know why you have been unable to fight my guards?"

"Because they have been doing this longer than I have and are better at it."

Smiling, he shook his head. "Not really. The reason you have been unable to succeed is because you try and strike before protecting yourself." Confused, she cocked her head. "Arwen, when you first entered my stronghold, what was your reaction to my guards?"

Taking a deep breath, she thought back to that day. "I wondered why people who could fight with magic needed weapons."

He nodded. "Have you come to any conclusions?"

Frowning, she thought about it. "Because their magic could blow everything up within a hundred miles?" At nights she had thought about it, imagining the damage two magical individuals could do to one another.

"Well, they could do that, true, but the answer is so simple, you are overlooking it. Remember, Arwen, magic is simple. Why would magical beings need weapons?"

Frowning, she imagined two of his guards doing battle. Each one's magic would bounce off the other's, neither one making headway. Slowly she sat up straight, looking him in the eye, "Because they can protect themselves against the other's magic."

"Exactly! When someone has practiced magic for a long time, it takes less energy than it does now. Once they get to that point, they can protect themselves magically from any but the most powerful magical beings. Which is why Grear was amused when you tried to hit him. I have the feeling your magic was supposed to be more than that flimsy object. What was missing?"

Grimacing, she explained.

His eyes twinkled. "If he wasn't protected, he would have been dead, because the power emitting from you was intense. I actually strengthened his protection a bit with mine to make sure you did not do something you would have regretted and not understood."

"Wait...you helped him?" Ari asked, her brain beginning to put pieces together.

"Yes."

"So, two people with magical abilities are stronger than one, if one is the conductor of the energy and the other shares their power?"

"Yes!"

"So, you want me to accept Terrian's help because..."

"Terrian's family are gifted protectors, Arwen. They aren't magical, per se, but nobody is able to get through their defenses. And I tried," he chuckled. "His eldest brother Lenorlin asked me to test them, and I besieged their family for three years. Only once was I able to get through and that was when their younger brother died and I found a fissure in their energy field. If he was on your side, it would give you added protection, protection you need to be able to fight off Orion." Squatting down, he stared right at her. "Arwen, you have an incredible energy field. Once trained, you will end up as powerful as I am. But you have a long way to go before you can build up that kind of ability. And quite honestly, you need Terrian's protection."

Shivering as the truth of his words hit her, she took a shuddering breath. "I don't want him to feel as though I am using him though. I-I like him."

"Of course you do, and anyone with a strong energy signature would be able to tell if you were honest or not. Tell him the truth. Invite him to Zeta. And before you quibble with me," he said holding up a hand to forestall her response, "tell him I told you to invite him. Be up front and honest. Tell him you cannot say the individual's name as he is able to track you in some way, but that Mayir would like him to come to Zeta for a meeting." Standing up, he nodded and in the next moment disappeared.

Huffing, she shook her head. This was happening so fast. Was she ready to meet Terrian yet? And if anything could destroy their budding relationship, this would surely do it. *Hey! Can you be my protection against a red-eyed demon who wants to own me?*

Whimpering, she turned back to the computer. Fine. The most important part of this was that she needed to fight off the bastard otherwise known as Orion. Even if Terrian wanted nothing to do with her after this was over, she needed to think of now. If Mayir was right, she was really strong magically and she could not even imagine that much power under Orion's control.

Hitting the reply button, she pushed back her

worries and insecurities and began to type.

Terrian,

>*I cannot say much as the individual who is after me seems to be able to find me too easily. The man who is training me would like me to ask you to come to Zeta to meet with him. His name is Mayir. If you can't, I understand. I don't want to interrupt your life or anything.*

>*And I feel stupid even asking, but if Mayir is right, and I have the annoyed feeling he tends to be right, it would be bad if this person got ahold of me, not just for me, but for everyone else.*

>*Anyway, if you are too busy, I understand, but if you could come, I would appreciate it. And...we could meet face-to-face, which might be kind of nice. I hope.*

>*Okay, signing off before I say something really stupid.*

>*Arwen*

Before she could regret and delete her words, she clicked submit and closed down the laptop. Since when did life become so complicated?

Oh, that's right. Ever since her sister, Jane, convinced her to go online. What she wouldn't give to be walking around Reid Park Zoo right now looking at Denise's warty pig.

Chapter Twelve - *Breakthrough*

"Try again."

Ari glared at Mayir as she once again hung from the ceiling by her feet due to the magical attack by two of his guards who were at the moment chuckling to themselves down on the floor. "I'm trying!" she hissed even as she tried to fight the sick feeling that hit her every time blood rushed to her head.

"It has been four days with no response by Terrian. We must assume he chose not to come," he said firmly. "As such, you have to get to the point where you can defend yourself. Now. Again!"

Grunting, she closed her eyes and imagined herself safe on the ground, right side up. Imagining wasn't hard, but she was in a bad mood and so when it came to feeling it, it just wasn't happening. "I can't do it!" A scream left her lips as the floor suddenly rushed toward her, but before she could ram her head into the hard stone flooring, she was standing upright, fighting the head rush.

"Stop that," she moaned, her hands holding her head which felt like the world was swimming around it.

When her head stopped pounding and she looked up, the two guards were gone and her dinner table had appeared with all sorts of wonderful delicacies on it. "Eat up, Arwen. We will begin again when you have restored your energy."

Slumping into her chair, she ate. Physically she knew the food tasted just as good as anything he had created for her, but mentally it tasted like nothing. Four days and no response from Terrian. She figured that meant he did not want to get involved and quite honestly, she didn't blame him. That didn't stop the disappointment she felt. A part of her had grown quite fond of him.

Unlike him, Orion kept messaging her. Each time she saw one of his messages, that pain in her chest grew a little more until it was with her even when she wasn't in front of her computer. Her body, her DNA, desired to go to him. It was sick, really. How dare her body betray her by desiring the sicko?

"Can the DNA he controls be removed?" she asked as she ate.

"No. There is no way to cancel the contract. Orion knew what he was doing when he captured Celie Agastion. He has enjoyed owning and torturing a woman of your lineage for almost five thousand years. It is what he knows. What he does. But you...you he wants for more than just that reason."

"You've mentioned that before. My energy signature makes me important. Could he really use me to do something horribly bad?" She had already figured out he could, but she wanted Mayir's input.

"Together, you two could destroy Zeta," he said in a clipped tone.

Turning her head, she stared at him as he stared out his one window. "But you refused to allow him back."

His eyes slowly moved toward hers. "Yes. But remember, Arwen, your magical ability rivals mine. When you reach your full ability, you will be my equal.

If you belonged to him, with the combined force of your magical signatures, you could shut dimensions, stop shifts, take over worlds if you wanted. You would be unstoppable."

Moving her eyes back to her plate, she continued to eat. It was worse than she thought. "So, he wants to take over things?"

He barked out a laugh as he turned to look outside again. "He is a being who does not like to be denied. Anyone who says no to him becomes his enemy. Orion is intrinsically evil, but then all beings from his realm are. The difference between them and him is that he learned to control magic and they did not.

"Arwen, I know this is a lot of pressure on you, but you must learn to protect yourself or you can never leave Zeta. I cannot allow such power to slip into his hands." Before she could respond, he disappeared. Obviously, their conversation was over.

For two days, he worked her from sunup until sundown, only taking tiny breaks to allow her to eat and use the restroom. Her body ached constantly, and her head was not in the game. A continual throbbing made it hard to think and almost impossible to concentrate. Finally, he shook his head. "You need a break. Go to your room and rest. I will devise something new for tomorrow."

Nodding, she turned and walked up to her room rather than trying to magic herself there. She dreaded to think what might happen. If someone was not in the right frame of mind could they get stuck part way between here and there? Or could something even worse happen like getting stuck in between transport in the middle of nothing? Hating the hideous nature of her thoughts, she quickly stripped out of the horrible outfit he had her dress in and sat down in front of her computer.

She booted it up as she closed her eyes, hoping the headache away. When the computer binged to let her know her messages arrived, she blinked her eyes open, having to blink them again as she was so tired everything was a bit blurry.

Two messages. Knowing they were both from Orion, she clicked on the folder, preparing to delete them. One was from him, but the other was from— "Terrian," she whispered, feeling hope for the first time that day. In a rush, she double clicked to open the message, not realizing until the message came up that she opened the wrong one. Staring in horror as Orion's face filled the screen, her eyes fell on the message at the bottom.

Now I have you. If you won't come to me, then I will come to you. Until you are mine, your pain will never go away.

Quickly deleting it, she fought to quell her rushing heartbeat. She hadn't meant to open up his email and now she wondered if he could have indeed figured out where she was because she did. If so, she should tell Mayir immediately. Unable to vocalize the intense amount of negative thoughts filling her brain, all she could focus on was the burning pain in her chest. How could he do that?

Taking quick, gasping breaths, she opened the message from Terrian. Whether it was good or bad news, she needed to read it.

Arwen,

I apologize. We had an emergency here,

*and I did not receive your message until today.
Let Mayir know I will be there just after the
sun reaches its zenith. I will bring with me
three of our special forces.*

Stay well.

Terrian

Well, the letter wasn't as sweet as his others, but
then again if he was busy and planning on coming here
tomorrow, then he probably had no time to waste.

"Mayir?"

"Yes?"

"I accidentally opened up a message from Orion
and now I am in pain. Plus," she rushed on before he
could reply, "Terrian wrote and he will be here
tomorrow just after the sun reaches its highest point."

"What did Orion's message stay?" he asked, his
voice right behind her.

"That he had found me and if I wasn't coming to
him, he would come to me. Also, until I accepted him, I
would be in pain." She rubbed at the incessant burn,
gritting her teeth against wanting to do something,
anything to stop it.

"That pain will be there for a long time," he said
quietly. "At least until he renounces his claim on you."

"He will do that?" she asked hopefully.

"He never has before, but then again, nobody
fought him like you either. If we are able to add in
Terrian's protection and our combined magic, you may
best him yet."

That wasn't very promising, but she tried to smile
in return.

"Rest, Arwen. Do you need me to bring you
dinner?" She nodded, knowing she didn't have the

strength to do it herself. "Fine." A plate of wonderfully colorful food, a bowl that held some sort of dessert, her consistently filling glass of water, and a glass of wine appeared in front of her. "Eat and go to bed afterward." Without another word, he disappeared.

As she reached forward to grab her fork, she happened to look down. "Mayir!" she cried, "I was still naked!"

His low rumbling chuckle resounded in her head. *"You just figured that out? You must be exhausted. Rest, child. Worry tomorrow."*

Hungrier than she realized, she basically shoveled the food into her mouth, taking gulps of water every few bites as her body demanded it be fed. After all the food was gone, she drank down the glass of wine and crawled into bed. Unfortunately, sleep did not want to come.

As her chest tightened and burnt, she knew she should be scared of Orion, but the thing her mind was fixated on was Terrian. Would he be attracted to the real her? At what point would she make an idiot of herself and turn him away? Could they even be the same people in real life? What if he actually had three eyes and his nose was on his chin? Well, no, she had seen his picture. Then an even worse thought hit her.

What if the rest of him wasn't like other human males? If he didn't have a...

Moaning at that horrible thought, she turned over and glared at the wall. "Seriously," she grumbled aloud to herself. "There is an evil demon who wants me to be his and is coming after me, and the thing I am worried about is if Terrian has all the right equipment?" Before she could continue her little rant, laughter filled her head. "Stop listening to me!"

"I would," Mayir responded, *"but you are extremely refreshing, Arwen. I have never met anyone quite like you."*

"I'm sure," she responded dryly, eliciting another chuckle.

Turning back over, she glared at the ceiling. She really could use some sleep, but her body obviously did not want to. Taking a few deep breaths, she thought about the next day. She definitely needed to put on some makeup, something she hadn't been doing since she had been on Zeta. Wait…she sat straight up and looked to the chair that would hold a new slutty Snow White costume within a few hours. Oh, no. There was no way she was meeting Terrian looking like that.

Well, if she couldn't sleep, maybe she could try and magic herself a cute outfit for the next day. Sitting up, she turned toward the chair, surprised when the room lightened a bit. So far she had not been able to tell where the light in the room came from and tonight was just the same. Must be magic.

Sliding her legs off the side of the bed, she closed her eyes, mentally sifting through her outfits at home while trying to come up with the perfect one to meet Terrian in. Her shorts were a possibility, but it seemed too casual to her. Then again, they were short and tight. Might be a great thing to start with.

Taking a deep breath to calm herself and trying to ignore the burn, she brought to mind her short stone-washed denim shorts and the yellow camisole top she usually wore with it. Once it was firmly in her mind, she forced herself to feel the material on her skin, not as easy as she hoped because the fact was once the clothes were on, she tended not to feel them at all. Finally, she focused on the feeling of pulling them on as well as how she felt as she looked into the mirror with them on. That would have to do.

Unfortunately, the pain in her chest elected to ramp up ten-fold at that very moment, and she never got to the third step. Instead, she let out a cry and collapsed onto her bed. "I hate you, Orion," she hissed through gritted teeth.

"I know you don't mean that, pet. And even if you do, it does not matter. You will want to obey me anyway."

His voice in her head made her jump from the bed, glancing around her. "Mayir!" she hissed. It took a few minutes for his voice to come to her sounding as though she woke him up.

"What is it, Arwen?"

"I just heard Orion!"

"Not a big surprise since you opened his message, and he probably pinpointed you here on Zeta. But remember, he cannot come here, so while he can taunt you mentally, that is as much as he can do. Now, go to bed."

Pursing her lips together, she placed her hands on her hips and glared into nothingness. Men! As though she could sleep between Orion's pain and voice and the prospect of meeting Terrian within hours.

Determined to have a cute outfit for the next day, even as she tried to ignore the fear that seemed to want to encroach, she once again focused on her clothing. Twice she tried and failed each time Orion came to mind. "Maybe I'm not picking out the right outfit," she said softly.

Instead of focusing on the clothing she owned, or had owned once upon a simpler time, her mind rushed through images of cute and sexy clothes she had seen in magazines. Almost at once, the image of an off-the-shoulder deep golden cashmere dress came to mind. Along with it were the heels and jewelry she would need to complete the outfit. This time when she got to feeling it, she imagined how it would feel to have Terrian's mouth drop when he spotted her.

The pain in her chest stopped, and with a smile, she floated through the last two steps. As she came down from what felt like a high, there they were. The dress, heels, necklace, earrings, and bracelet. "Holy cow!" she squeaked, slapping her hand over her mouth as her exclamation had been a little loud.

Excited at her recent success and not even interested in lying back down, she tried a few more outfits she had seen. By the time she finally crawled into bed, her room was covered in fine clothing she never would have been able to afford back home. This magic thing was useful.

****

Something wasn't right. She tried to move, but couldn't. None of her muscles obeyed her command. Even her eyelids would not open.

"All right, pet," Orion crooned into her ear. She gasped but as her lips were closed, no sound came out. She was supposed to be safe on Zeta. How had Orion gotten to her?

"You have been a bad little slave. Leaving me, not coming back when I commanded it, consorting with two of my known enemies. So, let's make this easy. Stay where you are at the moment. Relax."

Each of his words seemed to relax her muscles even further even as her head shouted *Run!* She had felt this before. The day she got sick and he took her without her permission.

"Don't do anything, pet. Just relax. They have been running you ragged, haven't they? Making you exercise your magical energy, energy you don't even understand yet. No need to worry, pet. I won't do that. I would never…harm you permanently. Are you tired of being pushed every day, pet?"

His voice was so nice and sweet, each note like a melody that wanted to carry her home. It never even occurred to her to fight it. "Mmhmm," she said, still unable to open her mouth.

"I'm sure you are. You know, there is a way for you to get out of it, a way to never have to deal with the pain and ache they put you through on a daily basis ever again. You can be strong, pet, oh so strong. I can help you."

Help her. He wanted to help her. No more being tossed into the air on an hourly basis, no more achiness. It sounded nice and she sighed.

"Yes, I hate what they are doing to you, pet. And all because they hate me. I am so sorry for that. They are abusing you to get back at me. And yet you have done nothing to them, have you?" Mentally she shook her head.

"No, you have not. Would you like to get away, pet? Away from them, the pain, their control?"

"Mmhmm." Even as the hum left her lips, something told her there was something she was supposed to remember, but what was it?

"It would be oh, so, easy," he whispered, his breath

washing over her ear. "I will help you, but you need to do one thing, just one tiny thing. Can you do that?"

"Mmhmm."

"Good girl." Something soft, a warm breeze, stroked her head. "All you have to do is say yes when I ask you a question. Can you do that?"

"Mmhmm," she responded, her mind feeling like mush. What was she responding too?

"No, no, pet. You need to respond with a yes, can you do that?"

Slowly she began to move her mouth around. It took all of her energy to do it. "Ysss," she mumbled, groaning from the effort.

"Ahh, good girl. Now, I will take you from here the moment you answer my next question. Do you hear me, pet? The moment you answer yes to the next question, they can't harm you anymore. Ever again."

"Mmm," she said, sighing in hopeful contentment. She didn't want to feel achy anymore, and her chest still ached. And her ankle was burning. Why was it burning? "Ankle," she tried to say, but it came out as gibberish.

"Shh, pet, you don't need to say anything else. Just say yes to the following, and they will never hurt you again." His lips touched her ear, and she shuddered even as her ankle burst into flames. "Do you accept your enslavement to me, pet?"

"Ankle," she said a little more forcefully. She wanted to grab her ankle and rub away the flames, but her muscles wouldn't obey. He needed to do it. "Douse the flames," she murmured.

"There are no flames, pet. Answer the question. Do you accept your enslavement to me?"

She heard the words and a part of her brain wanted to say yes in the worst way, but she couldn't concentrate on that. "Ankle on fire!" she screamed as her muscles seemed to wake up, and she jolted into a seated position, glancing around her even as she rubbed frantically at her ankle.

Mayir appeared almost immediately dressed in what looked like silk pajamas. "What happened?" he asked looking around. Even as he did, a hiss left his lips. "Orion!" he bellowed and in the next instant, he was gone.

Groaning, it didn't take long before the reality of her "dream" took shape. He had got to her; in the place she should have been safest, he found her and almost had her.

"Thank you," she whispered as her ankle continued to lightly burn. Immediately, she decided she needed to send a thank you note to the makers of that anklet. Whatever magic they put in that thing saved her butt more than once.

To say she got little sleep that night was an overstatement. The only sleep she had seemed to be a precursor to Orion's visit.

"How did he get in?" Mayir hissed for the seventeenth time since she finally stopped trying to sleep. Once she gave up, she dressed in a pair of dark skinny jeans and a T-shirt of her favorite rock band and joined him.

"I thought he wasn't allowed here," she said as she made a bagel and cream cheese appear in front of her.

"He isn't. There are barriers put in place to make sure he cannot enter our dimension. These barriers are strengthened daily. Someone is not doing their job." His eyes darkened and she was glad that look wasn't for her. It looked as though someone's head would be on a platter. "Verisha!"

The name sounded familiar and the moment the man appeared in front of them, she remembered who he was, the first individual she saw on this planet and the one who brought her here.

He cast a glance at her, smiling, before his smile disappeared and he turned. "Yes, Mayir?"

With a wave of Mayir's hand, every window glazed over and a small hum seemed to go through the room. "One of the barriers is down. I need you to check them inconspicuously. Find out who has not been doing their job."

"How could that be?" Verisha asked calmly. "And how do you know?"

"Because Orion came here last night and tried to spirit Arwen away," he growled waving at her.

Almost immediately, Verisha's expression turned to anger. "He came to Zeta? No! His filth will not be allowed!" He looked over at her, and while his expression calmed, his eyes did not. "Are you all right?"

"Uh, yes? Just didn't get much sleep." She wasn't sure how to respond to him. Who was he that Mayir would call for him?

Nodding, he turned back and bowed to her trainer. "You will have the zoor within the day." Mayir once again flicked his hand and the windows went back to normal even as the hum went away. Instantly, Verisha disappeared.

"Who...?" Ari began to ask, but Mayir stopped her.

"Do not speak of him. Nobody must know we suspect them."

The fact he spoke in her head while he was in front of her rendered her speechless for a few minutes.

"Terrian will be here within the hour," he said conversationally as she finished eating her breakfast. "I suggest you go do your preparations for his visit."

She took an hour to get ready, not because she needed it. She knew exactly what outfit she would wear, but because her mind kept going off in different directions, and it was hard to concentrate.

She started soaping up her arms and her mind drifted to the Orion fiasco. Twenty minutes later she found her left arm four inches thick in suds. Then as she shaved her legs, her mind switched to Verisha, and she was abruptly brought out of that thought as her skin burned because she was shaving the same area for the who-knows-how-many'th time.

After fixing her hair and pulling the cashmere dress over her head, she waited for Mayir to summon her. He told her he wished to speak to Terrian before she saw him to apprise him of the trouble.

Waiting was not easy. Was he here? How was he reacting? Did the dress make her chest look too big? Should she wear the necklace?

"Arwen, join us."

"It's time," she whispered as she straightened the dress even though it didn't need it and walked out the door. Sure she could have magicked herself down there, but quite honestly she needed the extra few seconds to try and stop the butterflies zooming around in her stomach.

Chapter Thirteen - *Dating Was Easy*

As Ari took the last step into the room, she immediately noticed the four new people. They looked nothing like Mayir and his guards. Whereas the men of Zeta were large, imposing, and radiated a strange purple aura she had come to recognize as their magical signature, the four newcomers looked much more human. If she didn't look at their uniforms.

Three of them stood off to the side dressed in charcoal gray pants that looked metallic and yet when they moved, they flowed like material. Their shirts consisted of a light gray weave that looked remarkably like crisscrossing chains. Covering their shirts was a simple black sash that went over their right shoulder. They stood at attention, a helmet tucked under their left arm.

Leaving them, her eyes fell upon the man standing next to her trainer. Instantly she recognized his face from the picture on the IDS website, but it was so much more intriguing in person. Dark black hair was pulled back into a low ponytail at his neck which emphasized his strong square jaw. From his jaw, her eyes glided up to his lips, which were a deep natural rosy red any woman on earth would kill for. High cheekbones and a straight nose drew her gaze, and for a moment she wondered how he had received the scar that ran from underneath his left eye to his left ear until she finally looked into his silver eyes.

They were looking right back at her and a smile curved up the corners of his lips. "You are even more stunning in person, Arwen," he said, a strange and yet alluring accent coloring each word. "The men in your dimension must be very happy indeed if all of your females look like you."

"They seem to want us to be anorexic Barbie dolls," she said in response, immediately wincing at the stupid line. Why had she never learned to accept a compliment? Terrian cocked his head in confusion.

Mayir snorted, though in all fairness it did look like he tried to hide his amusement. "I have spoken to Terrian about our little problem, and he assures me he is willing to help in any way he can, and considering the expression on his face, I can tell he means it."

Straightening up, Terrian sent him a quelling look, which just made Mayir laugh aloud. "Come, tell Arwen what is being done on your side," he said as he sat down on his chair.

Even though he had never once tried to make anyone feel comfortable in the room by getting them something to sit on, Ari wanted Terrian to be as comfortable as possible. Two minutes later a short lavender loveseat appeared as well as three folding chairs near the soldiers. She was quite pleased with her accomplishment until one of the soldiers let out a low chuckle.

"Stop!" Terrian said sharply and the soldier immediately stood straight and looked ahead.

"Is there something wrong?" she asked, looking at the three chairs. Then she saw it. One of the chairs was a kiddie chair. "Oops. I'm still learning," she explained, glancing between Terrian and his men. To her surprise, one of the men opened the kiddie chair and sat upon it, his back straight, feet on the ground and his head held high.

He turned to her with a solemn expression. "Thank you, my lady. It is rare that one is offered a seat in the house of Mayir."

She smiled tentatively at him before turning back. "Sorry," she whispered. Her mind had concentrated so hard on the loveseat that she barely even thought about the chairs.

"It was a kind thing to do," Terrian assured her. "My personal guards are not usually offered such accommodation. For now, though, I must ask them to leave so the three of us can have a private conversation." The one who had sat down stood up and all three of them saluted him, stomped their right foot once, turned, and walked out of the room.

That was strange.

"Shall we sit?" Terrian asked, waving toward the love seat.

Once she sat down, she was very aware of the man seated next to her. But she was afraid to say something and embarrass herself in front of both men. She was a constant source of amusement to Mayir as it was.

"I was explaining to Mayir before you came down how my family's protection works," Terrian began. "It is not as simple as just electing to protect someone. The protection our family affords its members and guards is granted through a ceremony known as the *Ishmara*. It is very sacred to us and unfortunately, we cannot just share it with everyone. However, there are things we can do to help you, Arwen."

As she listened to him, she took note of the way his voice would lilt on certain words, and how his mouth formed syllables. It was quite hypnotic. She had never met anyone like him before. Unfortunately, her mind was so caught up in what she was seeing she missed most of what he was actually saying.

"Arwen?" Her name brought her back to the here and now, and she realized she must have missed something.

"Yes?" Maybe if she tried to pass it off as nothing, Mayir wouldn't comment.

"She was too busy gawking at you to listen." And then again, maybe not. Shooting him a glare, she focused her mind on the here and now.

"I apologize. What was it you were saying?" she asked Terrian.

"I thought you and I should spend some time in each other's company. Once we get to know one another, I might be able to help you learn to deflect magical attack by lending you some of my protection. Once you figure out how to do it, you can then practice on your own."

"Oh. Sounds good." *And you, Ari, sound like an idiot.* Groaning inwardly, she kept a stupid smile plastered on her face. Maybe there was a dating service for the I-become-an-idiot-around-good-looking-men crowd.

Terrian held out his hand, and she hesitantly put hers into it, relishing the feeling of his skin against hers when he closed his fingers around her palm as they stood up. Before she could ask where they would go, as she knew Mayir would not give up his stone room, the room disappeared and once again they were in the dirt.

"Oh, very funny, Mayir!" she called, a rumbling chuckle his only response. She sent Terrian an apologetic look. "Sorry. He tortured me with this vista for two weeks. He has a sick sense of humor."

"Well, at least we are alone," he said with a smile, looking around. "It reminds me of one of the places I take Abriethon." Dipping down, he dug his fingers in the dirt. "Yes," he said standing back up. "Just like it."

"Well," she said, wanting somewhere comfortable to sit. "Would you like me to conjure some chairs? Or make some grass?"

"Whichever you feel up to doing. Or if you don't feel like it, we can walk."

Nodding her head, and hoping she did not make a fool of herself, she closed her eyes and imagined grass. But as Arizona winter grass came to mind, she frowned. It was so sharp and prickly. It would not be comfortable to sit on. Instead, her mind thought of the softness of a favorite stuffed animal from her childhood as she imagined the ground covered in soft green fur-like grass. Slowly, she moved through the steps, making sure she hadn't overlooked anything, and when she finally opened her eyes she burst out laughing.

As far as the eye could see, the ground was covered in bright green fur. Kicking off her heels, she rubbed her feet along it. "Yep, just like what I remembered," she giggled. She glanced at her companion who was smiling.

"Is this grass on Earth?" he asked, offering his hand to help steady her as she sat down.

"Not quite. The grass where I come from is prickly and uncomfortable to sit on. So I imagined one of my favorite stuffed animals from when I was a kid. His fur made me think of grass at the time." Her fingers stroked the ground. "Just like this."

"Before we get into what is going on, tell me how you found the Interdimensional Dating Service," he said, sitting down next to her. It wasn't until then that she actually noticed what he was wearing; she had been too fascinated by his face. His pants looked similar to jeans, though they seemed more expensive than any jeans she had ever seen. His shoes were dark gray leather and his shirt a dark gray button-down. He just seemed so human and yet, he wasn't.

"Well," she laughed softly. "Did I tell you much about my sisters?"

"Just a little."

Smiling, she told him about her family. "Well, my sister Cory is now almost fifty years old and she and her boyfriend seem happy. It is my sister Jane who is the most different of the three of us. She likes lists and planning and making sure everything turns out just so. Ever since Mom left, she has made it her job to get me married off. You should see some of the weird guys she has set me up with." As the words left her lips, she cast him a glance underneath her lashes. How many times had Jane told her a major rule was to never talk about past dates with a new one?

A large smile crossed his face. "Oh, I think I would like to. If they are anywhere near as strange as some of the dates I have been set up on, they are worthy of a story told well."

"Tell you what, let's trade off. I will tell you one and then you can tell me one." If they shared, it couldn't necessarily be bad. "I'll start off with my last Jane-approved date." She went on to describe Jay, from his beady eyes to his leers, before going on to his ability to chew and talk at the same time. By the time she got to his reference of her adult films—the ones that weren't adult—Terrian was laughing. But when she ended with the fact she got stuck with the bill, he stopped.

"The horrid man left you with the bill? No wonder you have not found anyone worthy of you. What a cad."

She smiled at his defense of her. "So, what date do you want to start out with? As you have been around for much longer than I have, I'm sure you have some doozies."

He leaned back on his hands and thought. "Ah, I know. My mother set me up with the daughter of a friend of hers. Kylea is from the Vilean Dimension. They are a very different race than my own—half my size, and the women have beards and mustaches. The evening was quite disconcerting."

The image of a female dwarf having dinner across from him came to mind, and Ari started to laugh.

"You laugh now. She insisted we go to a restaurant on her world." He paused, a distinct look of disgust crossing his face. "They do not eat the same things I do either." He cocked his head in her direction. "When you eat an animal, do you eat the inside or the outside?"

Jerking her head back in surprise at the question, she immediately answered, "Pieces of meat from the inside of the animal."

"Me too. Vileans think that is disgusting. They eat the skin, fur, and tail of the animal. Feet are a delicacy and…blood is considered better than wine," he shuddered. "Vilean bruckbeast is not palatable."

Giggling, she smiled. "I don't think I could have

done it."

"Our date was cut short," he said dryly.

"What's your world like?"

"Ahh, the Delania Dimension is made up of many planets, but as far as I know, ours is the only one that is habitable. Darinth is quite large with three continents. The one I live on is the largest and yet least populated. Our hamlet is the largest one on the planet. The library we live in is right in the middle of the city…"

"Wait. Library. I'm beginning to think that what you think a library is and what I think a library is are two different things." Remembering his messages, she was pretty sure of it.

He raised an eyebrow. "The building you live in is a house, yes?"

"Well, I lived in an apartment, but a building for one family is a house."

"A library is a very large house containing not just living spaces, but also a ballroom, kitchens, guest rooms for dignitaries…"

"Sounds like a palace," Ari said, her eyes wide. "Like where royal or really rich people live."

"Royal! Yes! My father is the crown prince, as such, we live there. Well, most of us."

"You live in a palace and your father is the crown prince…" Her voice drifted off even as her heart went thud. There was no way she had anything in common with a prince. IDS seemed crueler by the minute. Looking straight at him, she grimaced. "I'm nobody, Terrian. A simple girl from a simple town on Earth. I'm not good enough…"

"Good enough for what?" he asked in surprise. "For me? Arwen, my father may be the crown prince, but that does not mean I am in any way set for the throne. My eldest brother will receive it when my father steps down and then his eldest son after him. I work with technology, making sure our people have the best we can provide, but I am still just a nice guy. And I like you."

Her ankle tingled making her smile. "I like you too, but…"

He held up a hand. "No buts. We will get to know one another. If you like me, then the rest is just details. Now, what does library mean to you?"

They spent many hours talking out on the green fur until Mayir brought them back. It was a bit startling to be sitting on a comfortable blanket of fur one moment with the sun shining down on you and in the next be seated uncomfortably on a cold, hard floor staring up at him.

"Cute," she said, letting Terrian help her to her feet.

"The day is almost over. Have dinner and try to get some sleep. I have wrapped protection around the entire building. He will not get to you tonight. You and Terrian can talk tomorrow."

She turned to let her date know how much she enjoyed getting to know him, but with a huff, Mayir waved his arm and she was suddenly in her room. "Mayir!"

He never responded. "Old fuddy-duddy."

For three days, she was able to spend the daytime with Terrian even though the nights Mayir sent her up to her room the moment he brought them back. Sometimes he acted like an old mother hen. If he thought he was protecting her virtue, he was a decade too late.

On the fourth day, she elected to wear a pair of shorts and a camisole, much to her trainer's disgust. Terrian had not arrived when she went downstairs and the moment he saw her outfit, Mayir switched it to one of his naughty Snow White ensembles. "Stop that!" she snapped, switching it back.

"That outfit is not very ladylike."

"And yours is?"

"At least it covers your legs."

"Get over it. I have nice legs."

Their argument would have continued, but Terrian arrived, and the next thing she knew they were out on the green fur. "At least he left it this way," she said, sitting down with her legs crossed in front of her.

"In one of your messages, you mentioned chocolate. What is it?" he asked as he sat next to her. Each day he sat closer and closer and today his hips brushed hers as he took his seat.

"Kind of hard to describe. Might be better for you to taste!" Excited to share with him something she loved, she closed her eyes.

"Do you have to close your eyes to use magic?" he asked, interrupting her.

"Umm," she said, opening them. "I imagine better that way. Then again, I haven't tried it with my eyes open."

"That will come in time. Please, I am intrigued to find out what chocolate is. From the way you described it, it sounds wonderful."

Grinning, she once again closed her eyes. Wanting him to try a few different kinds of chocolate, she imagined a low table covered with mouth-watering chocolate. Molten-lava cake, chocolate pudding, strawberries covered in rich dark chocolate, each item she pictured made her mouth water. When it was as clear as she could get it, she moved on. After going through feeling the taste and scent of each delectable item, she quickly moved through the last two steps. Before her eyes even opened, she knew it had appeared. The scent hit her nostrils and she moaned.

"All of this is chocolate?"

Her eyes opened, and she stared gleefully at the large platter in front of them that held everything she had imagined. "Yep. Chocolate can be used in all sorts of food. This"—she grabbed the cake—"is the one I talked about in my email." After taking the closest utensil and filling it with the warm, gooey center, she handed him the spoon.

The moment the food hit his tongue, she knew he loved it. His eyes closed and a small moan left his throat. "That is divine. There is nothing like it on my planet. What does it come from?"

"A plant on Earth. I know there is a lot they have to do to the cacao bean to make it into chocolate, but whatever they do, it is so worth it."

They talked and laughed their way through the tremendous amount of chocolate. The only thing he wasn't sold on was the bowl of chocolate-flavored cereal, but that was fine with her. She ate them all. As the last plate was cleared and she leaned back, basking in the sun—it might not be as harsh as the Arizona heat, but it was still nice—a shadow crossed over her. She looked up at Terrian who was staring intently at her mouth. "What?"

"There is a spot of chocolate you missed," he said,

his voice taking on a tone that made her heart beat a little faster.

"Can you get it off?" she asked a little more breathily than she would have liked.

He leaned in and his lips softly touched the left corner of her mouth, his tongue sliding softly over her skin. There was a pause and then he kissed her again, this time, his lips slid a little further over hers. His soft lips were like velvet, and with a sigh, she wrapped her arms around his neck as she kissed him back.

Chapter Fourteen - *Magical Defense*

If it was the last thing she did, Ari would find a way to get back at Mayir. The jerk had waited until she and Terrian were making out and then transported them back into his stone room. Why he couldn't have waited an extra hour or two...? "Grr," she said, glaring at her wall as she tried to get over her embarrassment.

"It was all for the best, I promise you."

"Blow it out your nose, Mayir. You enjoyed that."

"Your phrases are bizarre, but I expect that from any granddaughter of Abigail. Believe it or not, I did not watch the two of you. I had no idea you would be so entwined. If I had, I would have brought you back several minutes earlier. But, if you are done sulking, Terrian has an idea I think has merit. Come downstairs and join us. And if you are not down here in five minutes," he added after a pause, *"I will bring you down here myself."*

"Insufferable," she muttered, going into her bathroom. Five minutes later, she walked down the stairs dressed in jeans and a T-shirt. Terrian was still dressed in his clothes from earlier. Instead of looking embarrassed, he smiled as she entered the room, holding out his hand as she walked toward him.

"Ignore Mayir. He gets so little fun," he said with a twinkle in his eyes. Relaxing the moment her hand touched his, she felt even better when he pulled her down onto the loveseat next to him. It still surprised her that Mayir had kept the loveseat around. "So, the two of us were talking, and we think it is time for you to start defending yourself against magical attack."

Frowning, she glanced between them. "But…I don't know how, and Mayir seems to love to watch me fail, time and time again, rather than just tell me."

Her trainer gave a large sigh. "Your failures, as you put it, are anything but. You learn much from each one. Since you are set upon being difficult, let me explain."

As Mayir went on to explain about magic and the impenetrable defense that could be created to fight it off, she seriously tried to pay attention. It was difficult to do while her ankle was thrumming quite happily—and so were other areas of her anatomy that rarely came to life.

"So, we thought I could lend you some of my protection to help you build your own," Terrian said. "This way you can learn how it feels, what it looks like to you, as well as how it feels to have a magical attack. Sometimes that is the most important lesson of all."

"Prepare her while I get four of my guard." Once Mayir left, she rolled her eyes.

"I still think he did it on purpose."

He chuckled. "More than likely, but he is trying to protect your virtue. As your guardian at the moment, it is his job. And try not to worry," he whispered, kissing her softly, "I plan there will be much more of this after we find a way around the Orion issue."

"Sounds good," she said, kissing him back.

"All right, I do not know how much time he will give us to prepare. We must get your defense activated before he returns. Come." He pulled her up from the

couch gently and walked her over to one of the walls.
"Close your eyes.

"I want you to focus on any strange feeling that
crosses your skin. My hands will be on your upper
arms, and I will give you some of my protective power.
Focus on any area that feels strange and tell me what
you feel." His hands wrapped tightly around her arms,
and her skin warmed up. Between the warmth of his
hands and the tingling in her ankle, at first she didn't
feel anything else. But then...

"There is something...almost a feeling of static
electricity surrounding my chest."

"Perfect, focus on that feeling. Let it grow and
expand across your body."

She had no idea how to do that. At first, she tried to
force the static elsewhere, but it stayed where it was.
Remembering Mayir's instructions about magic, she
imagined the static electricity surrounding her entire
body and then let it go. Instantly, the feeling spread to
every bit of her skin. "Oh, that feels weird," she
murmured. She could even feel it above her head.
Hopefully, her hair wasn't sticking straight up.

"Perfect. You are doing well, Arwen. Now, think
about this feeling. What color does it have?"

Color? How can a feeling have color? Realizing
she was being too logical once again, she focused her
mind on the static. As she concentrated on it, it began to
take form. Millions and millions of tiny lights glittered
off and on and, as she watched them, she focused in on
their centers, tiny balls glistening off the light. "Silver."

"Good. Now, I need you to be able to push it away.
In time, it would be best if it was about six inches away
from your body, but for now just try to move it a little."

Imagining the bright silvery lights pushed out about six inches from her body, she felt it and let it go. For a brief moment, they twinkled about six inches away before snapping back with a *whoosh!*

"That was fantastic!" Terrian said, hugging her. "You are a quick study. No wonder Mayir is so impressed with you."

Mayir impressed? Wherever did Terrian get that opinion? Not wanting to burst his bubble, she just smiled. "Can we try it again?"

They were able to practice it four times. Each time she was able to hold the light away from her for just a few seconds before it snapped back into place. Terrian thought it was an improvement. Her trainer did not.

"Only two seconds?" he asked with a frown. "Orion will be in your mind and capture your soul within three. Prepare." Without another word, he walked away and one of his guards, the one who loved to hang her from the ceiling, walked into the room. Annoyance and embarrassment at having Terrian see her like that made it hard to focus.

His soft voice whispered across her ear. "I am with you. He cannot harm you. Focus on the silver."

The guard leaned against the wall by the door looking bored. He kept his eyes on the floor and with a flash they looked at her. Immediately she felt her body begin to flip up but something held her in place. Looking down at her body she couldn't understand it.

"Concentrate, Arwen. Feel for anything brushing up against the barrier."

Remembering Terrian was helping her, she felt for anything strange. Almost immediately, she felt it. Like the sting of a papercut on her right thigh. "I found it."

"Good. Now," he said, his voice dropping to a very low level. "Focus on the silver around the sensation. Only in that area. Focus until that is all you see and hear. Then push it out quickly."

It wasn't hard to focus on the pain, but she had the feeling she was supposed to focus on the silver light. As she did so, she also felt something else. It was like a whirlwind building up within her. Her breathing sped up as she felt the little cyclone intensify. Not knowing what it was or what was going to happen, she figured she had better finish soon so she could ask. She imagined and felt the silver string push out and let it go.

A cry of surprise had her eyes springing open. The guard was hanging upside down from the ceiling with a look of shock on his face. A giggle of surprise left her lips as she felt the light spring back into place. As it did so, he dropped, twisting and landing on his feet easily.

Mayir nodded at him and he scurried out. "What was that?" he asked her, an eyebrow raised.

"What do you mean? I did everything Terrian asked." She turned to look at the man behind her, and he was looking at her with something akin to awe. "What?"

"At your level of training, Arwen, you should not have been able to disarm his magical armor. I told you, you were powerful. This proves it. What happened?" Mayir's question both worried and excited her. Maybe she did have a defense against Orion. Of course, if she gave into him, she would also be a major weapon.

"I'm not sure how to explain it. He told me to feel for something odd against the light, and I found it. Then he said to focus all my energy on it and push that part of my defense out right there. As I was focusing, I felt what I can only describe as a cyclone build within me. When I pushed it out, I felt the whirlwind go too. At the same time he cried out and, well, you saw what happened."

The two men looked at one another and then back at her. "Try that again, but without Terrian's influence." Before she could ask what he meant, Terrian walked a few feet away and the very first guard she'd met when coming here walked in the door. Not once had he shown her anything except disgust. What she wouldn't give to see another expression on his face.

Knowing if she didn't concentrate, it could all end before it began, she focused on the light. Instantly she felt his attack, like huge claws ripping across her abdomen. Ignoring the pain, she focused on the silver, seeing Terrian's eyes in every dot, but the whirlwind didn't come. Figuring that had been a one-time thing, she still concentrated on pushing out the area of the light and let it go.

As she opened her eyes and looked up, all three men watched her. The goon had a frown on his face. Well, at least it wasn't disgust.

"Was anything different?" Mayir asked.

"No power build up this time."

He waved a finger toward Terrian, and he walked up behind her, wrapping his arms around her. "Again," he told the guard.

The feel of the claws intensified, but her mind couldn't concentrate on that as she felt the building storm in her chest. There it was. Keeping her mind somewhat on the silvery light, she focused on building and intensifying the tornado. It whipped faster and faster inside her until her chest began to feel tight.

Instantly, she imagined the barrier pushing out right where the claws were. As she let go, Terrian whispered, "Green, furry grass."

Her eyes flashed open as she looked over her shoulder at the same time she heard a huge yell and a large *boom* filled the room. As Terrian began to shake with laughter, she looked around trying to find out what happened. A large hole was in the wall, and something green was crawling out of it. It wasn't until cold eyes met hers that she realized the man who had treated her so disdainfully from the beginning was covered in the green furry grass from the field. A little giggle escaped her lips even as Terrian let out a huge guffaw.

The clearing of a throat brought her attention to Mayir who actually looked as though he was trying not to laugh. "Well, that question is answered. Vres, I think you should wear your new skin for a while, until you realize just because someone is smaller than you does not necessarily mean weaker." With a grunt, Vres walked out, bowlegged from all the grass. With a snap of Mayir's fingers, the windows went opaque and the humming started.

"Tell me what happened," he said eagerly.

After Ari described what happened with her, Terrian added his piece. "I can feel when she lets go, and when she did it, I mentioned green, furry grass wondering if that distraction would make the effect less. I did not expect," he chuckled, "for it to become a suggestion."

"Intriguing. You two are a formidable pair. Her magic and your protective energy, Terrian—Orion might have actually met his downfall."

Things became more interesting and a lot more fun

after that. Not only was Terrian constantly holding her, but he came up with the most bizarre suggestions for each practice attack. Of the seven magical attacks she dealt with over the next two days, one became a bird, one a mouse, two ended up wearing dresses, two were sent to the green fur field, and one disappeared and nobody knew where he went.

"You are doing wonderfully," Terrian assured her as they took their dinner in the fur field away from Mayir. "Mayir may not show it, but even he is impressed." Tonight she magicked up a simple dinner of steak and baked potato, and he dug into it with relish.

"I'll just be glad when it's over," she admitted. "I don't like this constant shadow looming over me."

"I know and to be honest, I want to invite you to Darinth after all of this is over. I think you would like it." His eyes twinkled. "And we have a library that should please you. Over two million books are housed inside it."

"Yes, but I doubt I could read a word," she laughed.

"I think you would catch on. For one thing, teaching through visual media has been a way of life for us for thousands of years. Most of the books are picture based. I would also like to take you for a ride. Abriethon misses me I am sure, and he would love nothing more than to give my lady a ride."

"Your lady?" she asked with a smile.

His eyes softened. "I was not going to bring this up until the problem with Orion was solved, but a Darinthan knows within a short time when they have met the one who was meant for them." He took her hands in his. "You are the one for me, Arwen. I know you have other things, more important things, on your mind right now. But know that once it is over, I want to take you to Darinth, hopefully to make it your new home."

****

Do guys really talk like that? Later as she sat brushing her hair before bed, she wondered. It was obvious they must since Terrian had bared his soul to her just an hour earlier. It had been wonderful hearing how he described his thoughts of her, and she was partway somehow there with him too already. She could see herself with him. And that scared her. Logical Arwen Maria Reynolds couldn't fall for some guy so quickly. So why was she already in love with him?

"He's a prince, dummy," she muttered, hating she had to remind herself of such a major obstacle.

"You think too much." Mayir appeared in her room, frowning. "This isn't Earth or even worse, the Cragort dimension, where people are judged by their bloodlines. Terrian's family are good people and will welcome you with open arms if you let them. Besides, you do not even know your true lineage. After this thing with Orion is behind you, ask Abigail about it. You may find you have more to offer Terrian than you know. Your grandfather is very well respected."

"You've mentioned him before. Who is he?"

"No, you won't be getting that information from me. That is for Abigail to tell you. For now, try to sleep. Tomorrow you start a new round of training."

"What now?" she whined making him shake his head.

"Yes, you and Terrian can defend you from a known attack, but you must get used to the unknown."

Without another word, he was gone.

"One of these days, I am going to make you give me a straight answer."

He chuckled. *"I look forward to the day when anyone can make me do anything."*

Curling up in her bed, she smiled. True, she had a madman after her, but had her life ever been so fun and so fulfilling? There was a part of her that would miss this once they figured out a way to get Orion to back off. She was sure her life would go back to boring...unless she followed Terrian to Darinth.

****

"Again."

Growling in annoyance, Ari glared at Mayir. "Five times I have been attacked without being prepared and five times it has hurt Terrian who had to rush to try and protect me from it. There has to be another way or more information you haven't given to me, yet. Cough it up."

"Once again, your way of speaking brings forth rather hideous mental images. Have you not figured it out yet?" he asked in actual frustration. She had never seen him frustrated before. "You must be prepared at all times for an attack. At all times. It does not matter if you are in the shower, out for a peaceful walk, eating dinner, or kissing Terrian. You. Must. Be. Prepared. Some part of you must be aware of your buffer at all times, so when a magical signature attacks, you are aware of it before it can take control.

"Do you think Orion will sit back and wait until you feel him to attack?"

Wincing at the force of his words, she shook her head. Of course he was right, but she was frazzled. She had now been working almost completely nonstop for

185

weeks to find a way to keep Orion at bay, and she needed a break.

"No, of course he won't," she whispered. "Mayir, I'm burnt out. I need a break! I can hardly think, let alone concentrate. It feels like I'm going crazy."

Shaking his head, he turned and looked at Terrian who nodded and stood up. "I will be back," he said calmly and left with one last look at Ari.

"Arwen, I know you are afraid of him, and you have heard of what he can do, but you do not know the depravity to which that zoor will go," Mayir said through clenched teeth.

It was true, she didn't know. But on one hand, she wasn't sure she needed to. He was bad. She got it. No matter what, she needed to figure out a way to keep the bastard at bay. She got it. Abigail's words came back to her. *"Ask Mayir about it once you have been there for a while. You never piss off one of the fae folk. Never."*

"What did Orion do that got him banned from Zeta?" During her time here, she had tried to get to know the enigmatic man in front of her, but his aloof exterior made it difficult. That and the fact his attitude was maddening.

His jaw tensed for several minutes before he physically relaxed. "It is not something I like to talk about, but you deserve to know. Do you remember Verisha?"

"The man you sent to check out things a couple weeks ago?"

He nodded. "He has disappeared."

Her mind whipped through what little knowledge she possessed of the time she listened to them. "Do you think he is the traitor?" Someone had let down the barriers that protected Zeta, and somehow Orion had got in. It would be disappointing if it was Verisha. He seemed so nice.

"No! He would never put us in peril that way. It was the two of us together who put the barriers in place centuries ago. No, my fear is he went after Orion himself."

While she wanted to egg him on, she knew he said things in his own time. If she tried to push, she might not hear it at all.

"He was mated to my daughter Leonaya. They were very happy and gave me the most delightful granddaughter anyone could ask for. Sharya was happy. She laughed and played all day, and as she grew, she became an incredibly superb young woman. Until the day she met him.

"You see, Orion had skiffed our dimension many times over the millennia, causing small problems, but nothing big. He was like a Vrillian tongue beetle. Annoying, but not enough to worry about. For over a century before the…event, he tried to get our females to follow him to his realm. But they were too smart for him. Enough complaints came to me that I asked him never to return.

"On our world, that kind of request is taken seriously, Arwen. Other beings accepted it, left, and never returned. I thought he did the same. Until the day my daughter contacted me, frantic because Sharya went missing."

As he spoke, Ari curled in on herself. She knew she did not want to hear what happened to Mayir's granddaughter and yet that she had to.

"He never even tried to cover his trail. He wanted

me to know who took her."

"He made her into one of his slaves, didn't he?" she asked in a tiny voice when he stopped talking.

"Worse. He did not want her, Arwen. He wanted to show me he was more powerful than I was. He stuck her in a dark space and never let her out, taking delight in tossing things at her and scaring her whenever he could. Verisha and I went after him. Three months we followed his trail. We shifted again and again, jumping dimensions as we followed his energy signature.

"One day, Leonaya contacted us. Sharya had been returned. Of course, immediately we went back." His voice, which had been steady and somewhat dead, turned ice cold. "Her body was there, but her mind was gone. He broke her by torturing her mentally until she could no longer take it. She was only sixty years old. She died in her mother's arms three days later. Two weeks after that, Leonaya took her own life. Verisha and I spent a good century going after Orion, but he was and is very good at staying hidden, and the realms protect their own. Unable to go after him, we did the only thing we could. We protected our people."

Silence rang through the room even as tears stung her eyes. Slowly, he turned to face her, his expression that of one who had lived through too much. "Arwen, I know it seems frightening, but I will not let you go through what Sharya did." He mumbled something else under his breath, but she didn't catch it. "If you are too tired to continue, look at that bedroom as your jail cell. For you will never leave this building. He *will not* take you."

His words rang through the room with utter finality, and she nodded, knowing she would have to find the strength to continue. Before she could say so, the door burst open.

"Mayir! Arwen!" Terrian called, running into the room. "Abigail is coming. I just spoke with her. Something is dreadfully wrong."

Chapter Fifteen - *Decision Made*

"What is it?" Mayir snapped, his face losing the tired look it just held.

"She wouldn't say," he said, pulling Ari into his arms where she lay her exhausted head against his chest. "All she said was plans had changed and it would be up to Arwen how she handled it."

"How long?"

"Two hours."

"Stay with her." Without another word, Mayir left the room, barking out orders in a language he rarely used when Ari was around.

"This is bad." Ari's words did not need to be spoken. Even before she felt Terrian's nod against the top of her head, she knew them to be true. Orion had done something to force her hand. He could have taken Jane or Cory, and she could not hide away in Zeta if that was the case. Even the thought that one of her sisters could end up like Mayir's granddaughter made her physically ill. Happy-go-lucky Cory with her positive view of the world, reduced to a mindless body. Or Jane... She hiccupped as she wondered what would happen to Jane's children if he destroyed her. Taking a deep breath, she pulled out of Terrian's arms. As much as she would have loved to stay there and hide from the world, she couldn't do it. Orion wanted her. Well, she would just have to rely on the training she had to get her through.

"You have decided." The words were quiet, his silver eyes sad.

"If it has brought Abigail here, it must be bad. I won't let anyone else suffer. I can't."

Nodding, he stood back. "Practice."

As she took her stance and prepared her defenses, defenses no longer supported by his energy as neither of them knew if he could accompany her where she was going, he went to the door and called in a few of the guards to test her.

Anger. Deep-seated anger filled her up. Fury at the being who was so selfish he destroyed others for his own happiness. No, not his own happiness…his amusement. Rage rumbled in her chest as the guards faced her and attacked in ones and twos. None of them was able to get through that thin web of light that surrounded her, but she wasn't able to overcome their defenses either.

"Enough!" Mayir said, walking back in where Ari stood covered in sweat as she faced her newest challenge. Three of them at the same time. "Abigail is five minutes away. Arwen, drink something." A large glass of water appeared in her hand and she chugged it down.

As Terrian came over and put an arm around her, she kept drinking. How did a simple girl from Tucson become the individual who would fight such a horrid creature?

The guards left and neither of the men talked as she took deep breaths and tried to calm herself. Any moment, Abigail would walk through that door and tell her one of her sisters was in that bastard's clutches. As much as she tried to prepare herself for that, she knew she couldn't. It would be a blow, a huge shock, and she wished she could make her mind accept it before hearing the words.

Abigail rushed into the room, her eyes frantically searching for and spotting her granddaughter. "Arwen!"

"Abigail!" she wailed, throwing herself into the arms of her grandmother. "Which wo-one? Which one did he take?" she gasped out.

"Calm down, Arwen," Abigail said sharply. "Get a hold of yourself. You need to before you hear what I have to say."

Her lips trembling, she pulled back, relieved when Terrian wrapped his arms around her, giving her as much support as he could in that moment. After a couple deep breaths, she nodded and looked her grandmother in the eye. "Okay. Did he take J-Jane or C-Cory?"

Abigail's pale face fell. "Neither one, honey. But…this is going to be hard to hear. Are you ready?"

Confused, Ari nodded. If he didn't take Jane or Cory, who could he have grabbed? Surely not Destra. So few people even knew where she was. Leaning against the one person in the room who felt solid to her in that moment, she nodded. "Tell me. I will only make up worse and worse scenarios until you do."

Nodding, Abigail took a seat, her hands slightly trembling. "I'm sorry, Arwen. I had no idea he would do this. If I had, I would have taken them myself and hidden them away no matter how much Jane thinks she can protect them."

Wait. Jane? Who would Jane protect? Even as the question came to her, Arwen began to tremble. "No!"

she screamed, knowing exactly whom Jane would protect at all costs. "NO!" Her entire body fought to get loose, struggling against the unmovable arms that held her still.

"He took Kari, Nellie, and Shasta," Abigail continued in a shaky voice. "Cory contacted me as soon as Jane called her. Orion took them right in front of her. One moment she was putting them down for naps, the next he appeared, told her who he was, grabbed the girls, and they were gone."

"No," Ari said, tears falling down her face. Her delightful nieces. He took them and would turn them into mindless bodies. No! She couldn't let it happen. No! "Where can we make the exchange?" she demanded in a much calmer tone than she would have expected considering how she was feeling. "He wants me? He's got me! But he has to give those girls up first unharmed."

"No!" both Mayir and Terrian said at the same time.

"I have to." Turning her eyes to Mayir, she saw how he struggled with this. He knew what was possible if she went to Orion. But he also knew what was possible if she didn't. And she would not let her nieces go through that.

Rubbing one of the arms that held her tightly, she watched her grandmother. "When is the exchange?" she asked again.

"He told Jane he would send someone to negotiate. No time was set."

Nodding, she managed to turn around in Terrian's arms and bury her face in his chest. It was so much worse than she expected, and she thought she had expected the worst.

"You should rest," Mayir said in a somewhat kind voice.

Quickly, she pulled away from Terrian and shook her head. "No. I have to be ready for anything. I have to be able, not only to defend myself, but to deny him at the same time. My nieces are being held by a whacko who thinks it is fun torturing people. I will *not* rest until they are safely home with their mother." Even if that meant losing herself.

She doubled, tripled, and even quadrupled her efforts to fight off magical power. There wasn't enough room in the stone room, so she went outside and demanded the guards magically attack her from their posts. They turned to Mayir as if asking for his permission. With one nod, it started.

Excruciating pain. The attacks came at every part of her protection, some pounding, some slicing, some digging into it. But she would not give up. Terrian kept offering to help, but she refused. "I won't have your help then, I can't take it now."

Hours upon hours of constant attacks without respite and, with a scream, she finally dropped to her knees and pounded on the ground. "HELP ME!" she screamed, actually hoping something in the universe would respond. Tears poured out of her eyes and blood poured from the numerous cuts and scrapes caused by the magic she was unable to push away.

"Arwen," Terrian said in a hoarse voice as he never took a break from going any further than five feet away from her during the ordeal. "You do not have to do this alone. Please! Let me help you."

Sniffling, she shook her head. "What would it

help?" she asked sadly, looking up into his pain-filled face. "I have to do this on my own because when it comes down to me versus him, there will be nobody to help me. If I can't do it now, I won't be able to do it later."

"There must be a way!" he exclaimed, shaking his head. His hair had come out of its binding many hours before and swung freely around his anguished face.

****

"Arwen, I command you to take a break."

She turned to Mayir in fury. For over two days, she had practiced, only taking small breaks to eat and sleep. "It was you who told me I couldn't take a break. And you were right! If I'm not prepared, he will…" She had a hard time articulating all the horrible things he could do to her nieces, but when he shook his head sadly, it hit her. The sad truth she did not want to face. "He won't give them up until he has destroyed them, will he?"

"No, he won't. Our waiting for his negotiator is just a tactic. He has time on his side, and he knows it. In the meantime, he will *play* with their minds."

"I have to leave." As Terrian began to shake his head, she shook hers in response. "Terrian, I have to leave Zeta and go somewhere where he can find me. If we wait for his terms, the girls will be worse off than dead, and I will have to live with the knowledge that I could…I could have stopped it," she managed to choke out. "I need to know how to get to his realm."

"No," Abigail said, saying something for the first time since she had informed Ari of what was going on. "If he gets you in his realm, his power is stronger. You cannot go there, Arwen. You have to meet him somewhere neutral."

She was exhausted, so tired she couldn't even think straight, but she nodded anyway. Ari had already accepted her fate. In fact, she accepted it the moment she found out who he took.

She knew if she told them, they would fight her on it, but she saw no other way. She would accept the enslavement if he would deliver the girls safely to their mother.

From the sounds of it, her mind would be a thing of the past soon enough anyway, so she wouldn't have to mourn the loss of her family and of Terrian for long.

If there was only a way to destroy Orion in the process.

Unable to move, she wasn't surprised when she found herself in her room under the covers on her bed. Too tired to make a comment or even to care, she closed her eyes, the only thing she could see behind her eyelids were the sad eyes of a Darinthan male whom she had come to care for far too much.

It took another day before she was able to regain enough energy to get up, get dressed, and walk to the stone room. Strangely enough, she felt calm. Her mind had already decided. Today was the day, and they would just have to let her go. Terrian, Mayir, and Abigail looked up as she entered the room.

"How do you feel?" Terrian asked, rushing to her side.

"Ready."

A strange shudder went through him, but he nodded. Pulling her in for a hug, he held her close. "I know why you have to do this," he whispered to her, "but I still wish you would let me help."

"I won't let him get you, too." The last thing she wanted was for Orion to get hold of a new toy and have that toy be someone she loved. She had the feeling he would torture him in front of her, and she would not be able to handle that.

Mayir watched her, but did not say a word. His face looked haggard, and she wondered if he felt as though he had failed. "It isn't your fault," she whispered. "You have done more than anyone else to get me ready."

"It is my fault, but you will never know why," he said with a sad smile. "I will send you to where he can find you when you have said your goodbyes." Without another word, he turned and walked out of the room.

Terrian hugged her close. "This is not goodbye," he said harshly in her ear. "You will see me again." Pulling her head back, he kissed her roughly, passionately, showing her physically the words he dared not say aloud. And then, he was gone.

He released her, the pain in his face something she would remember until she could remember no more, and then turned and walked away, his shoulders slumped forward as he strode from the room.

Slowly Ari turned and looked at her grandmother. It was her plan to leave. It was her decision, and she accepted that as the adult she was. But in this one instant, she felt like a little girl who just wanted her Nana to take it all away. A sob escaped her throat and then another one.

Abigail strode forward and pulled her sharply into a hug.

She cried for a long time, letting every feeling she had loose as she held on. When the tears began to dry up, she said what she needed to say. "T-tell Cory and Jane that I love them, that I'm sorry I will never see them again. Let the girls know about their crazy Aunt Ari, okay? Please don't let them forget," she said with a sob.

"Nobody will ever forget you, Arwen," Abigail said in a husky voice. "But don't give up, honey. You can come back to us. Please, come back to us." They held on for a few minutes more before Ari knew if she did not pull away now, she might not be able to.

A commotion in the yard made them both turn toward the door. Arwen's heart sped up. The negotiator must have arrived.

Instead, Mayir, Terrian, and Verisha walked in the door.

"Verisha!" she exclaimed, happy he was back and alive for Mayir's sake.

He looked at her, his eyebrows rubbing together. "You have been through too much already, young Arwen."

"I'm glad you are back. Mayir was worried."

He raised an eyebrow and looked at his father-in-law. "You must be slipping if you let someone know your true feelings." He just got a glare in response.

"I am glad you are back, Verisha," Abigail said with a forced smile. "Mayir wondered where you went. Once Arwen has gone, maybe you can tell us the tale?"

"Arwen is leaving?" he asked in surprise.

"She is going to face him." Mayir's words hung heavy in the air, and Verisha looked around in surprise.

"Then I came back at the right time. I bring information," he said simply, "on how you can beat Orion."

Chapter Sixteen - *The Contract*

"Yes!" Terrian exclaimed.

"You know how to beat Orion? How?" Mayir demanded.

"Sit, sit," Verisha said, magicking chairs out of the ether for all of them. "Do you want the long version or the short one?"

"Short one," Ari said. "I have to go free my nieces."

His head snapped up. "He has your nieces?" She nodded and a strange keening sound left his lips before it cut off. "What you need to know is there is a holding place where all magical contracts are kept if the purveyors of said agreements wish to have recourse if someone breaks it. This place keeps the magic intact, even if those who originally created it lose their ability to do so on their own. To place a magical contract within the archives, you must have within the contract a way of ending it at some point. Mayir and I assumed all these centuries that Orion would not have been stupid enough to place his contract there."

"You found it," Terrian said, his eyes darting to Ari's with hope. "How does she get out of it?"

"It is a simple and not so simple thing. Written at the very end of the contract, obviously as his way of getting it recorded, was one line. 'To end the suffering of those within the Agastion bloodline, the one he asks must deny him thrice.'"

Silence filled the room as Ari ran the words over in her mind. "What does that mean?"

"It means you have to say no to his request that you accept his enslavement," Mayir told her. "Three times."

"I've already said it once. Screamed it actually." And it had hurt like hell. Could she deny him twice more?

"Does it have to be three times in a row? Or three times over time?" Abigail asked, leaning forward.

"I don't know. The escape clause was short and gave no other information."

"That's okay," Ari said, letting out a long breath. "The fact is, there's a chance. Which is a thousand times better than what I had fifteen minutes ago." She stood up. "But still there is no time to waste. Mayir, I need you to send me now." She still felt fear. Seeing Orion again terrified her. But she also felt hope. From the sounds of it, if she said no three times…"Wait. Does that mean if I can say no three times all the females in my family are forever free from his control?"

Mayir chuckled. "It certainly sounds like it. The zoor must have added that line without thinking it through first. Good! First bad mistake he's made." He turned to Ari, an expression on his face she could not understand. "Ready?"

Slowly she looked around the room. Verisha watched her without an expression on his face, Abigail with hope, Terrian with love and worry. "I'll be back," she whispered, unsure if she believed it but hoping it would be true. The last thing she saw before the room disappeared was a single tear dripping down Terrian's cheek, following the path of the scar that she never got the chance to ask about.

Bright light shown all around her, and she blinked, squinting to get her bearings. As she looked around, she was startled. "What are you doing here?"

"I will take the girls to safety."

She hid a smile. He might never admit it, but she thought Mayir had a bit of a soft spot for her, probably hoped to help as long as he could. "Thank you." *For everything.*

He just nodded. "Follow me. We are on Drega Prime, an almost uninhabitable planet. This is the safest place to bring you as Orion should feel cocky about being here. Nobody to anger while he is being a zoor."

"I've been meaning to ask," she said as she followed him along an almost imperceptible path at the base of two hills. "What does zoor mean?"

He chuckled lightly. "It started out as a rather rude nickname for people from his realm, but over the millennia has come to stand for any being that has no goodness in them whatsoever."

The area around them was barren. The hills were dead gray dirt, and she couldn't see a plant in sight. "What happened to this planet? Obviously we can breathe, so there's a decent enough oxygen atmosphere, but why are there no plants?"

"The peoples who used to inhabit this place destroyed it through their greed. They created poisons that destroyed their own land. Finally, they had to move on to another planet when they could not grow enough food to survive. They are currently destroying it now."

"That's kind of sad."

He barked out a laugh. "Have you not noticed,

Arwen, beings who should be intelligent tend to not be so when money or some sort of gratification is hung in front of their face? Even your own planet has its problems, hmm?"

Grimacing, she nodded.

They walked several miles at least before they came up on a large plain. Gray dirt was visible everywhere she looked. "We wait," he said when she looked at him.

So this would be where she battled Orion. Would he bring the girls with him? Would she get to say goodbye before Mayir took them to safety? In a surprise act of emotion, he put an arm around her and squeezed. She winced as some of the hairs on the back of her neck caught on something, but the pain was negligible considering the action.

Before she could respond, the air seemed to *whoosh* around them and there he was. Standing fifty feet away, Orion watched the two of them. He was dressed in the same clothes he had worn in the coffee shop the first time she saw him. "I don't want you, Mayir," he said with a sneer. "Go home like a good little Fae."

Mayir growled softly but did not respond. Ari decided it must be up to her. "He's here to take the girls home to safety. As I won't be able to," she tacked on, hoping he would get what she wasn't saying. Both Mayir and Orion turned and looked closely at her. "I'm sorry," she whispered to Mayir as she took a few steps away.

"Hmm," Orion said, watching her. "But they are such good little assurances, my pet, though they are very annoying. How can three little humans be so incredibly loud?"

Her lips twitched, but she couldn't really feel amusement. "Take it or leave it, Orion. Either bring the girls so he can take them or I leave now and you will never find me again." It was as big a bluff as she had ever made in her life, but she hoped he bought it. When he didn't move but kept observing her, she took a step back toward her trainer.

"Wait," he said. "You won't leave if I give the little brats over to your babysitter?"

Her mind went over everything. If she agreed to stay, that wasn't agreeing to his enslavement. "I will stay here if you bring the girls and give them to Mayir."

Nodding slowly, he was gone.

"Where did he go?" she asked, afraid she had blown it. Would the girls pay for her mistake?

"He went to get your nieces. He doesn't have the ability to send others unless he is with them." Mayir turned and looked into her eyes. "His greatest fault is his ego. He thinks he is more powerful than he is. Use that any way you can."

As she nodded, the air changed around them again and he appeared, the three girls lying dead on the ground at his feet. "No!" she screamed, ready to dash forward. Unable to move, she realized Mayir's magic was holding her in place. "Let me go!"

"No. Not until he releases the girls from their slumber and sends them with me."

Slumber? They weren't dead? Relief went through her. Orion gazed at her mentor with disgust. "Take them. They are of no use to me." In the next instant, all three girls lay around Mayir's feet.

He looked at the three of them and then up at her.

"Good luck, Arwen Maria Reynolds Agastion. Remember everything I've taught you." Before she could respond, they were gone and she was left with Orion.

Never in her life, not even when she was wandering along that straight rode on Zeta, had she ever felt so alone. Standing just a few feet away was the enemy. Was she good enough to fight him? At the thought, her mind seemed to instinctively trace her light barrier, becoming aware of every shift and change in it.

"So, pet, we meet again," he said smoothly, walking toward her. "You kept me waiting a very long time. You should be proud of yourself. Nobody in your bloodline has ever done that before. Of course," he continued, "you will be punished for your disobedience. First off, you have a question to answer, do you not?"

A tug at her right hip made her aware it was happening. He had started his assault. Focusing on that area, she gently pushed it out and away, not wanting him to realize just how much she had learned.

"Question? I wasn't aware you asked one."

His red eyes darkened, and a grim smile crossed his gaunt face. "Playing games, pet? I almost had you twice, but something tore you away from me. Not anymore. This time you will answer me."

A burn began in her ankle and started its way up her leg. As she shored up her protection, she backed up as he advanced. "Once again, I'm waiting for a question."

"Fine," he said, stopping his advance and flicking something off his slacks. "Pet, do you accept your eternal enslavement to me, your master?"

Just like that, it happened. Attacks on several areas

of her shield happened at the same time. Panicked, she was unable to focus, and he made his way in. Immediately, her chest tightened and breathing became difficult. Her brain went fuzzy, and she had a hard time remembering what was going on.

What was she supposed to be doing?

She needed to breathe.

There was something important she was supposed to be doing.

"Air!" she gasped, "I need air."

"Say yes, and you can have all the air you want," he said in a deep soothing voice that she so desperately wanted to follow. As she dropped to her knees, grabbing her neck, her left ankle seared with pain, and for a brief moment in time her head cleared.

"NO! I won't accept—" Her voice cut off as breathing and speaking became impossible. Her chest tightened even more, and her throat seemed to shut off.

"No?" he hissed, standing over her. "So you enjoy choking, pet? Fine, I will let you choke until you pass out. When you come to, I promise you will be more malleable. It will be easier to gain your respect back in my dungeon anyway. So many torture devices I can use on you."

At the word dungeon, images of blackness entered her head, and she knew she had to fight. If he got her back there, the chances of her getting out of this were nil. Struggling to stay on her knees, she tried to ignore the need for air and the incredible desire within her to give into him, even as she worked at strengthening her protection.

It was so hard, black spots began to swim in her vision, and she didn't know how, let alone what she should do to repair the holes in her silver barrier. At the thought of silver, Terrian's eyes swam in front of her face. "Come back to me," he said and with a strangled interior cry, she fell over.

Terrian. If she passed out, she would never see him again. Ever. She would live a life she wouldn't wish on anyone. Plus, if she could somehow fight Orion off, she would free her family forever of the zoor. Her hands moved to the back of her neck, clutching each other, even as she rolled her body into a ball.

Think! Think, Ari! What do you need to release his control and get some air?

Power. Cyclone. She knew that kind of energy only came when Terrian held her, but it was her only hope. Reaching down, she grasped hold of her ankle even as she brought him to mind. She felt him holding her, the amazing power within his arms, and the way he lit her up when he kissed her.

"Hurry up and pass out, pet, I have plans for us once you accept," Orion said, interrupting her.

Just like that, anger coursed through her veins. Orion had enslaved women in her family for five millenia. And now, he planned to enslave her? Energy began to twirl in her chest, and she trembled. Plus, he had kidnapped her three nieces just for fun. The power built, pushing her chest out and in, and she realized with relief she was breathing. Without the fear of passing out, she concentrated on the openings he made in her barrier, mentally repairing each one in preparation for what she was about to do.

There would only be one chance, and if she screwed it up she would have wasted all her energy on this one attempt. He would have her because her barrier would collapse. But she had to take the risk. "Ask me again," she demanded in a raspy voice, struggling up to her knees.

His eyes narrowed as he walked around her. "How are you breathing?" he murmured and then paused. "Ahh, my pet is ready to accept. That would be the only reason the pressure would let up." Taking two steps backward, a cold, hard smile crossed his face. "Pet, you will be my slave for the rest of your days. Do you accept?"

There it was, the final question. She hoped denying him three times over time fulfilled the escape clause, because she had nothing else in her. She let all the images and memories of what he had done fill her up. Kidnapping her, her nieces, his twisting of Celie her great-great aunt, and finally his destruction of Mayir's granddaughter. Fury burst from within her as the cyclone in her chest seemed to take over her body.

Opening her eyes, she stared right into his, thrilled to see them widen in surprise. "For the last time," she said through parched lips. "No. I *do not* accept your enslavement, you red-eyed zoor!" At the last word, the power burst within her breaking through the fissures he created at the same time as a strange image passed quickly through her head. With a groan, her body collapsed as a scream filled the air.

****

The sun pelted down upon her as she lay on the dirt, but she had no energy to get up. Her breaths came hard and fast, and when something came between the sun and her, she whimpered. A male voice cleared its throat, and it did not sound like Orion so she cracked an eye open. Standing above her was a man with one eye and two noses. Surely, she was hallucinating. She closed her eyes and reopened them to be sure. Yep, one eye, two noses. "Who are you?" she asked, coughing at her dry throat.

"My name is Circe Olendeerthal," he said in a nasal voice. "What is your name?"

"Ari." Oh what she wouldn't do for a glass of water. Even as she thought it, one appeared in front of her, and she guzzled it down. As it refilled itself, she drank it down again. By the third glass, her head felt a little clearer, and she sat up and looked around. "What happened to Orion?" The last thing she remembered was exploding.

"Ah, so you were with Orion when the contract was nullified, yes?" he asked, pulling a large stack of papers from his briefcase.

Just like that, her brain put the pieces together. "I did it. I nullified the contract. I said no to him three times!" Laughing in shock, she laid back on the dirt.

"It would seem so," he said with a frown as he held the paperwork. "Do you know where he is?"

"Uhhh, no? The last thing I remember is telling him no and things went dark for a while."

"I see. Well, Miss Ari, you have created an incredible amount of paperwork for our office. We have to release every female in your DNA strand. Do you have any idea how many that is? It will take us a century to find them all." He sighed and ran his sleeve over his forehead to capture sweat that wanted to drip into his eye. "Anyway, if you see Orion again, could you tell him to get in touch with the magical contract archives? He owes us for all this new paperwork." He stuffed the papers into his briefcase and stood up.

"What a horrid planet. Do you live here?"

"No. I need to get back to Zeta, actually." How long had she been gone? Did time go at the same rate from here to there? Where was Orion anyway? He could have taken her even though she said no. It wasn't as if she was in any condition to fight him off. Considering how horrid he was, he didn't seem like someone who would honor the end of a contract if he could find a way around it.

"Ah, well, I will leave you to that, then. I have to make a report of all this," he sighed, looking around at the dirt.

"Uh, well, if you must," she said, slowly rising to her feet.

"Oh, yes," he nodded emphatically. "I must. All 'I's must be dotted and all 'T's must be crossed, you know."

"Sure," she said, even though she had no idea what he was talking about. How would he report dirt, anyway? Shaking her head to get rid of such a strange concept, she realized she had no idea how to get back to Zeta. "Crap."

"Pardon?" Circe asked, pulling a pencil out of his pocket.

"I don't know how to get back to Zeta."

"Ahh, that is your problem. Now, I must get back to mine." Without another word to her, he began to walk around, making notes of whatever it was he thought he saw in the dirt.

Frowning, she looked around. Why had it never occurred to her that she needed to find her way back? Oh, right, because she never actually thought she would get back. Walking a little ways away from Circe and his annoying note taking of nothing, she cleared her throat. "Mayir? If you hear me, I'm ready to come back." Nothing happened.

"Ugh." Spotting hills in the distance, she began to walk toward them. Maybe if she got back in the area where they arrived on the planet, she could contact him easier. Hours later, she had no idea if she was close, and she was hot and sweaty. The sun was going down. Not good.

So, how did I get from my bedroom to the stone room? It had been simple really, once she figured it out. All she had to do was imagine herself in that room, feel how it felt…just like Mayir taught her. Pausing, she cleared her mind and focused on the stone room. She felt the coolness of the stone and saw the light coming from the windows. Mayir was seated on his chair, morosely staring into nothing. With the image in mind, she drifted through the other steps.

As the warm moist air dissipated and dry cool air took its place, she opened her eyes. She was definitely in the stone room, but nobody else was there. "Mayir!" she cried, running outside. The sight that met her gaze was bizarre. Mayir's guards were gone, not one of them in residence, and in the center, between four of the flower patches, Mayir and Verisha were sparring. With sticks.

"You can't seriously expect to hurt one another with those," she said in exasperation as she walked up.

Surprised they both turned to her. Mayir's face broke into such a large smile, she was surprised it didn't crack his face. "Arwen!" he called, leaping over the flowerbed between them and pulling her close. "You bested him!"

Beaming, she nodded. "Yep! The contract is now null and void! And Orion seems to have disappeared. Where is everyone?"

"Abigail took the girls home, and they seem no worse for their journey, by the way. Orion might have put them to sleep immediately as they do chatter incessantly, don't they?" Verisha said, walking up. "Glad you did it. Terrian will be thrilled."

"Where is he?" she asked looking around, hoping to see a set of silver eyes.

"He had to return to Darinth at the command of his father. We told him we would let him know as soon as we heard something, though. I suggest you get some dinner, maybe wash off all that dust," Mayir said, looking over her, his normal demeanor setting back into place, "and then we will take you home. Go."

Chapter Seventeen - *A Great Start*

Arwen looked at her reflection in the full-length mirror. It was hard to see the woman in the mirror as the last three days zoomed through her head. After taking Mayir's advice—well, it wasn't so much advice when he sent her directly to the shower in her room—subtlety was not one of his gifts. After taking a shower and putting on a pair of shorts and a T-shirt, she ate a salad and then went down to the stone room.

Verisha was gone, but Mayir stood waiting for her, dressed in jeans and a button-down shirt. "You're looking very human," she remarked, waving at his clothes. Her eyes widened as she took in his ears, which had lost their pointy tip and looked very human.

"Earth does not know of the existence of the different dimensions, and we would prefer to keep it that way," he explained simply. "Earth is a very backward place. The last thing we want is any of them finding out how to find us. It is best if I fit in."

"Are you going to Earth?"

"Of course. I am taking you there. Are you ready?"

"Yeah, but…" Before she could continue, the stone room was gone, and in its place was the small round room with the insignia on the wooden floor. "Cory!" she screeched, running for the door, Mayir momentarily forgotten.

"Ari!" Cory yelled, opening the door. In the next

instant Ari was grabbed and swung around by her sister, their laughter bouncing off the ceiling. "Ah, hell, sis! We were afraid we wouldn't get you back!"

"Me too!" she said grinning. Cory looked over her shoulder, her eyebrows raising. "Oh," she gasped, turning around. "Cory, this is Mayir, my mentor, trainer, and all around good curmudgeon."

"Her manners could use some work," he said dryly as he stepped forward. "Ms. Corrine Reynolds Agastion, I am Mayir of Zeta. It is a pleasure to meet another of Abigail's granddaughters."

Frowning, Ari looked at him. Why was he so correct all of a sudden? Then she caught the longing look in his eyes. Ooooh! He was attracted to her sister. "She has a boyfriend," she said, garnering a frown from the two of them.

"As usual, dear girl, you are reading things wrong," he responded before turning back to Cory. "Is Abigail here?"

"She went to see Mom but should be back any time. Jane is bringing the girls over soon. They will want to see their Auntie Ari," Cory said with a wink at her sister. "They can't wait to tell you about the strange man with red eyes who kept talking about you."

"Ugh," Ari said with a shudder. "He is the last one I want to hear about."

As Cory led them from the room, Ari found as her toes touched the edge she felt a little fear about stepping over it. She was safe in this room. Once she stepped outside of it...

"He's gone, Arwen," Mayir reminded her. "The contract is void."

"Yeah, but we don't know what happened to him

when he left," she hissed, peeking around the corner. "What if he is just waiting to try again?"

"You conquered him the first time, and you will conquer him again," he answered simply, following her sister down the stairs.

Must be easy just to put it out of mind like that. Taking a couple deep breaths, she checked her shield and found it intact. *Good.* Forcing herself, she stepped over the threshold. Nothing happened. Sighing in relief, she followed them to the first floor, taking a seat in her favorite rocking chair, which unfortunately put her in the hot seat as she realized all the other chairs in the room faced it.

"Okay, I'm sure you don't want to tell all in front of the girls, but I want to know what happened," Cory said the moment she sat down.

"I, too, would like to know what happened."

"Well," Ari said, chewing on her bottom lip for a moment, "I will tell you, but I think it won't sound nearly as weird as it actually was." Haltingly at first, but then moving on with more strength as she remembered it all, she told them. "It was strange as I felt the power build. It wasn't something I was used to without Terrian holding me and yet...somehow I did it."

Cory, who hadn't said a word the whole tale, smiled. "Oh, Jane is going to go crazy about this Terrian person. When do we get to meet the stud muffin?"

Ari began to laugh even as Mayir said, "Stud muffin?"

"Ignore their way of speaking, Mayir. It will just confuse you," Abigail said, charging into the room.

"Abigail!" Ari said, leaping up and hugging her grandmother.

Hugging her back, Abigail beamed at her. "I knew you could do it. Your energy is very intense."

"She had some help," Mayir said, almost sounding affronted.

"Of course, we know you helped train her," Abigail responded, waving her hand at him. "We won't forget your help."

"That is not what I am talking about. Terrian was with her in spirit if not in body."

"I did imagine him there," Ari admitted. "But usually the cyclonic power thing didn't happen without him."

"As I said, he was with you," Mayir said calmly.

"What do you mean?"

"That is for him to explain when you see him. Which you will need to do as soon as possible."

Huffing, as she knew that would be all she would get out of him, she turned toward Cory. Before she could say anything else, her sister spoke up. "How long is she staying?" The fact she asked him and not her was quite annoying.

"She can only stay here for a couple days at most. And while she is here, she cannot leave your house as everyone here thinks she is dead."

"Hello! I'm right here!" she said, feeling a little forgotten, and that feeling was a bit unsettling.

Three individuals gave her a strange look and then went back to talking as if she wasn't there. Thankfully, Jane and the triplets arrived moments later, and she was able to concentrate on them. The girls didn't seem any worse for their kidnapping, in fact they had very few memories of it.

"The man wif red-eyes took us 'cause he said he needed you, Auntie Ari," Nell explained once the three stopped screaming in excitement when they saw her. "He said you would save us and you did." She beamed showing where her front teeth were missing.

"What happened to your teeth?" Ari asked, worried he had done something.

"They fell out last night. I got two whole dollars from the tooff fairy," she said, grinning widely.

Being back with family was nice, but something was missing. She wanted to see Terrian badly. "Is my laptop back on Zeta?" she asked once Jane and the girls left.

"No," Abigail answered. "We destroyed it so that Orion had no chance to trace you ever again."

Her mouth gaped for a moment before closing. How could she contact Terrian and let him know she was okay? "Does he know I'm back?" she asked, hoping they would know who she meant.

"I'm sure he knows you are gone from that planet," her grandmother responded, thinking of the wrong he. "I wish we knew what happened to him."

"Me too," Ari said, wrinkling her nose. "I still do not understand where he went. It isn't as if he would have left me there if he had the strength to take me. So something must have happened."

As the four of them discussed the event, she began to relax, and questions she had thought of before came to mind. "Abigail," she said when there was a lull. "Who is my grandfather?"

Mayir actually looked amused even as Abigail raised an eyebrow haughtily. Cory looked on with interest, as it would be her grandfather as well. "Why do you want to know?"

"Oh, please," Ari sighed. "Mayir told me my magical signature was as strong as my grandfather's."

"I also told you it was as strong as my own," he commented.

Ignoring him, she went on. "He won't tell me who it is, so I am aski—" Her words stopped even as his words went through her head. So many times he mentioned she was as strong as he was. Why had she never made the correlation before? "You?" she gasped. "You are my grandfather? Why didn't you just tell me?"

He dared to look affronted. "You mightn't look so put out about it, Arwen. I gave you many clues. You just weren't paying attention."

Glaring at him, she truly wished she could get back at him. He just smiled at her. Now that she was thinking, other things began to make sense. "Orion knew, didn't he?"

Frowning, he slowly nodded. "I think so. Your magical signature is very close to mine. He hates me so entirely, finding that within you was probably more than he could ever wish for. Yes, he wanted you, Arwen. For you, alone, are very powerful. If he had use of your power, he could destroy me." The words were spoken calmly, but the force behind them would have knocked her over backward if she wasn't sitting down.

"You know, in a way that makes me feel better."

Cory snickered at Ari's words even as he looked at her blankly.

"I could never figure out why me. Now I know, it wasn't me. It was you. Pointy-eared freak," she added with a giggle. He might be annoying as hell, but now she understood why he wanted to protect her so badly. Part of it might have been the magic, but it was also the fact she was his granddaughter.

Sighing, Mayir shook his head and turned to Abigail. "Your granddaughters truly have no respect."

Laughing, Abigail nodded. "Just like me, hmm?" Shaking his head in mock annoyance, his twinkling eyes gave him away.

They continued to talk until late in the evening when Cory set up a mattress in the small oval room at Ari's insistence. "I just don't think I could sleep anywhere else," she admitted sheepishly.

For two days, she answered questions, rehashed the meeting with Orion into infinity until finally she had had enough. "I need to see Terrian!" she said in exasperation when Mayir and Abigail were embroiled in a discussion of how to stop this from ever happening to the women in her family ever again.

He raised an eyebrow. "Well, why did you not say so before? I have been waiting until you were ready." Her eyes narrowed and she glared at him. Leave it to him to make it her fault. "Your glare is pitiful. Maybe you should spend some time with Vres, he has it down to a science."

So here she was. She spent over two hours getting ready, scrubbed her body until it shined, took special care with her hair and face. Without thinking about it, she magicked a silver halter dress onto her body to finish the job. After creating some sandals to go with it, she walked out of Cory's bathroom and into the little safe room. The three of them were waiting.

"Are you going with me?" she asked in surprise.

"Nope," Cory laughed. "I don't want to stop aging. I'm keeping my feet stable on earth, thank you very much. Besides, Brent would miss me if I left."

Hugging her, Ari squeezed. "I will contact you. Maybe send you some strange things like Abigail does."

"Cool. Find me one of those penis deities. I would love to tease Jane with it." After another hug, where Cory had a hard time fighting back tears, she left, closing the door behind her.

"So the three of us are going."

"Wrong again," Abigail chuckled. "I will come to the Delania Dimension soon and visit. I wish to get to know this man of yours. For now, I have a few things to do on my home world."

"And I must return to Zeta. Verisha found the one who did not keep up his barrier, and we must deal with him quickly."

"So, I'm going alone?" Ari asked surprised. "Will Terrian be there to meet me?"

"Highly doubtful. More than likely his father will meet you." Before she could do so much as freeze in fear, the room disappeared, and she stood in what looked like a foyer of a grand hotel—high ceilings, marble-like flooring, and tall columns. Deciding she would really have to find a way to hurt Mayir at some point, she looked around for the front desk.

There wasn't one.

"Miss Arwen Reynolds Agastion?" Ari turned toward the voice and saw a slightly older version of Terrian standing a few feet away, dressed in what could only be called regalia. A white jacket buttoned over deep gold pants. Several medals were hooked on the right side of his chest. His hair was black with silver at the temples, and he had the same twinkling silver eyes as the man she loved. Uh-oh. *Please let this not be the crown prince.*

"Y-yes? I'm Ari."

His lips smoothed out into a smile as he stepped forward and took her right hand between both of his. "It is a pleasure to meet you, my dear. Terrian has not stopped talking about you since he got back. I apologize he was unable to meet you, but considering the danger, he is sequestered until he gets his protection back." He pulled her hand into the crook of his elbow. "Come, I will take you to him."

Confused, she followed him through a large doorway into a huge room with white stone flooring. There was no furniture in it, so she had no idea what it was for. On the other end of the room was a grand staircase. As they began to ascend, she asked, "What do you mean 'until he gets his protection back'? He had it when I was on Zeta. How did he lose it?" Surely, nothing bad had happened to him. He was fine when she left. Panic began to build in her chest. With his protection gone, Orion could have gotten to him. In fact, all of those guards could have gotten to him.

He paused on the last stair and turned to her. "He did not lose it, dear child. He gave it to you."

Her eyes widened as she heard his words. "What? But..." She couldn't verbalize her crazy thoughts. Giving up his protection was crazy! Anyone could have attacked him. But he gave it up to save her. And it worked. Tears began to prick her eyes as she remembered the last time she saw him with that tear dripping along his scar. "How did he do it?" she whispered.

He chuckled and shook his head as he climbed the last stair and walked down a long hallway to their right. One part of her brain noticed the opulence of everything around them. The clean white wainscoting on the walls, the gold leaf wallpaper and the art that was more than likely priceless. The rest of her brain was focused on what Terrian had done for her.

"I will let him explain. To be honest, he refused to tell us. We have been waiting to hear of you, to know that his protection worked." He winked at her as they reached a double door at the end of the hallway. "Finding out three hours ago that you were alive and well and coming to see him was a great relief to us all."

He opened the two doors and waved her inside. When he did not follow her, she turned around. "I will see you later, Ari. It was a great pleasure to meet you. My son has chosen well." Without another word, he closed the doors behind her.

Whoa. So, he was the crown prince. Should she have curtsied or something? Frowning, she turned around, surprised to find herself at the beginning of a long hall with no doors on either side. At the very end was another set of double doors. She walked toward them, glancing at the strange designs in the walls. She wasn't sure what they were, but they were pretty. They reminded her of natural flowerbeds that weaved and twisted amongst themselves. In no time at all, she reached the other end. Should she knock? Or just walk in?

She chose to knock. Without a noise, the doors opened, and she came face to face with Terrian. "Arwen!" he yelled, pulling her into his arms faster than she could even react. "It worked, it worked," he muttered, pulling her through the doors. Before she could ask him any of the number of questions she had, his lips met hers and she forgot everything but him for a long time.

When she came out of her haze, she was curled up next to him on a long light gray sofa looking out floor-to-ceiling windows. A huge forest stood in the distance beyond a sea of buildings. Turning to him, she smiled. "How?" That was all she wanted to really know. How had he transferred his protection to her?

He smiled and his hand reached behind her neck and she winced as her hair caught on something. The memory of the same thing happening with Mayir came to her and her eyes widened as he pulled his hand back and she spotted a small silver piece that glinted like metal in his palm. "What is it?"

"When I knew you were prepared to give yourself up to save your nieces, I knew I had to give you the only thing I had, my protection, to hopefully keep you safe. When I went outside with Mayir, I told him what I wanted to do. Members of my family are born with this innate protective barrier, while the rest receive it upon going through the *Ishmara*." He pulled away for a moment. "Watch my neck." Confused she focused as he pulled his hair out of the way and placed the silver disk on the lower part of his skull. Instantly it seemed to melt and become a part of him. Within a minute, it disappeared. He gave a small shudder and then smiled. "I had never been without the protection before. I have to admit the last few days have been difficult."

"Mayir did it," she said, shaking her head. "I wondered why he put his arm around me. Now I know."

"Well, he wanted you to succeed as much as I did. Did it help?" His silver eyes latched onto hers and she smiled.

"I had no idea how to beat him," she admitted. "I said no, and he got through my defenses when I panicked." He stiffened and she continued quickly. "I couldn't breathe but knew I had to do everything I could. So, I focused on the memory of your arms around me and felt the power build. I thought it was just the memory of you that did it. But now, I know why the power was as strong as it was. I concentrated on anger, on everything he had done, and just let it all out when I said no for the last time. Your protection allowed me to breathe when I thought I would pass out. It helped me keep a level head. You were with me even though I didn't know it," she laughed softly, leaning her head against his chest.

"Oh, Arwen," he sighed. "I am so glad it worked. What happened to him?" Something in his voice made her look up.

"I don't know and that is a bit of a worry. I used all the energy I had at the end and was unable to move for a long time. When I finally was rousted by an inter-dimensional lawyer type, Orion was gone."

A small chuckle left his lips. "Well, you did have my protection and power. Think of anything interesting right before you let it loose?"

Frowning, she tried to remember. "Wait! You know what happened to him."

Grinning, he shrugged. "Well, no, I do not, but if it worked, it serves him right."

"What?" she asked, wanting to know what could

have happened to her enemy.

"I added on a slight suggestion into the protective field when I removed it. I hoped, just like when you turned Vres into a furry green monster, that it would work."

Pulling back, she looked straight at him. "What did I do to him?"

"Do you remember an image or a thought hitting you just as the energy left?"

Cocking her head, she ran through the events. "Yes. There was something. It came so fast the first time I didn't get a hold on it. Even seeing it now, I don't understand what it means." An image came to mind of a small black slug-type insect slithering along a bright yellow trail.

He jumped up and rifled through some images on a nearby desk. When he turned around, there it was.

"Yes!" she cried, jumping up. "That's what I saw!"

Laughing, he handed her the image and sat down. "That is a Vrillian tongue beetle," he snickered. "I overheard some of what Mayir told you and this image came to mind. It sounds like you turned him into one."

"Oh my God," she said, starting to laugh. "So he's crawling around in the dirt?" She wondered if Circe had found him. He might be a noteworthy thing to find.

"Maybe. Or you might have transported him to the wades in Vrill. That is where the Vrillian tongue beetles make their home. We can hope that is the case, because the wades give off a natural energy that denies anything magical. So, if he is there, he cannot magic himself back into human form until he crawls out, and if he is there, it will take him, oh, a few centuries to achieve. That is, if one of the beasts who feeds on them does not get him first."

Laughing in relief, plus thinking that was a suitable form for him to have taken, she collapsed onto the sofa next to him. "Oh, it's kind of a relief. A part of me was afraid he would appear at any moment."

Chuckling, Terrian put his arms around her. "Arwen, now that I have you here, I need to ask you something." Looking up, she was surprised at the seriousness of his tone and face.

"Okay." Would he ask her to leave? She couldn't blame him if he did. He had been through a lot since they met on IDS.

"Do you love me?" The four words were simple, but her eyes widened. "Because I love you and I need to know if you feel the same way."

This was awful fast. They just found one another online, met, kind of dated while Mayir helped her and then…shaking her head at the logic that wanted to control her actions, she took a deep breath. "I…uh." Why was it so difficult to express how she felt about him?

A low chuckle rumbled in his chest. "Yes, I have studied Earth dating customs. They are strange," he mused. "You date for years before you are willing to share your short lives with one another. A Darinthan knows within a short period of time if he or she has met their mate. I knew the first time you fed me chocolate how I felt about you." She smiled at the memory. "In fact, I have requested some of our scientists to learn everything they know about cacao production and how to turn it into chocolate. This continent has tons of room to grow it, and it would be a great addition, I think." He placed his finger underneath her chin and prodded it upward. When she looked into his eyes, he stopped. "I know you are worried, but I hope you will at least be willing to 'date' me. Though, I dearly hope you will not make me wait two years to make you my wife," he grunted. "I will have to protect you constantly."

Stunned, she blinked. "You want to marry me?" How had they gone from love to marriage? Butterflies bounced around in her stomach even as her left ankle began to tingle and the feeling slowly spread up her leg.

"Of course," he responded in confusion. "Did I not make that plain? I love you, Arwen. Finally, I have met the woman I wish to be with me for the rest of our lives. I know and, once you know, my mother will plan the *Ishmara* and we can wed. Then…"

As he talked, the tingling sensation began to take over her whole body. Immediately Abigail's words came back to her. *"About seven centuries ago, they entered into a contract with the Interdimensional Dating Service to provide magical talismans to their female clients to help them recognize men they might truly match well with."*

Laughing softly, she reached down and stroked the raised crisscrosses. Since she had gotten the anklet, she had mostly noticed the burning as it warned her off Orion, but she remembered now all the nice feelings it gave whenever she read Terrian's emails.

"It knew even then," she whispered.

"What knew what?" he asked, watching her hand.

Looking up at him, she gazed into his eyes. "It knew what you meant to me," she said smiling. Reaching forward, she kissed him before pulling back. "I do love you, Terrian. Marriage is a huge step, and I would like some time to get used to it. But I do love you, and I want to be with you."

A smile spread across his face. "That is a great start, my lovely Arwen. A great start."

Chapter Eighteen - *Epilogue*

Giggles and laughter reached Arwen, and she smiled as she gazed at her reflection in the mirror. One year ago, she had been fighting for her life against a psychotic zoor. Today she was marrying the love of her life. Her fingers drifted over the back of her neck, trying to feel and yet knowing she wouldn't, the thin piece of myr metal lying at the base of her skull. The night before she had gone through the *Ishmara* ceremony and was given the eternal protection of Terrian's family.

But today, she would get to see her family, well most of them anyway. Abigail had assured all of them the travel between dimensions wouldn't hurt her nieces as they were growing and children were not as affected by shifting as adults were. Unfortunately, Jane could not come as she was happy with her husband and children and did not want to tempt fate. Cory, in her own words, had said, "To hell with it. If I stop aging, Brent can just crow he has the youngest woman around. I'm not missing my baby sister's wedding."

"We're here!" Abigail called as the door to Ari's room opened and three girls ran in laughing and squealing. Kari, Nell, and Shasta were dressed in simple spring dresses. Ari thought they looked adorable.

"Auntie Ari!" they screamed as they caught sight

of her. "You're pretty!"

Laughing, she reached down and hugged each one. Terrian's mother Ishlie had become a good friend to her. Even at over one thousand years, she kept a youthful playfulness that made Ari laugh. Before her family arrived, Ishlie helped her dress in her ceremonial wedding gown. Not having to shop for a wedding dress had actually been a plus in Ari's book. It would have been too difficult to choose a gown that would perfectly match the love she felt for her soon-to-be husband. The sleeveless silver gown felt like silk. It hugged her bodice tightly, but flowed out at the waist. The only decoration on it was a gold sash that went over her right shoulder. A tiara of spun silver topped off the ensemble. She truly felt like a princess.

"Well, so are you," she assured her nieces. "And I am so glad you can be a part of my wedding."

"Smile!" She looked up to a blinding flash as Cory took her picture. "Ooh! I promised Jane I would document everything," she smirked.

Chuckling, Ari reached forward and hugged her sister. "I've missed you." As her sister pulled back, she finally saw her grandmother standing behind them. "Abigail, I'm so glad you came."

"Ah, honey, wouldn't miss it. Besides, Mayir is going to be here in his finest clothing, which from what Verisha tells me was considered fashionable about six millennia ago. I had to come or I would miss the ability to get something to tease him about for the next few millennia," she snickered, hugging her granddaughter.

"Ah, your family arrived." Ishlie, crown princess of Darinth walked in, looking regal in a similar dress to Ari's. It was the twinkle in her eye that belied the royal figure in front of them. "Abigail, it has been a long time," she gushed, reaching forward to hug Ari's grandmother.

Cory raised an eyebrow at her. "Abigail knows everybody, I guess." Snickering, Ari nodded.

A tug at her skirt made her look at Shasta. "Who's that?" Shasta asked in a loud whisper. "She's pretty."

Ishlie turned and smiled, her brown hair highlighted with silver streaks waving as she laughed softly. "Well, thank you for the compliment. Are you Nell, Shasta, or Kari?" she asked, squatting down in front of the little girl.

"Shasta."

"Well, you are very pretty too. You and your sisters will look amazing in the wedding procession. I am so glad you could join us for your aunt's wedding to my son, Terrian."

Now that the ice was broken, the three girls chattered at the tall lady in front of them as if they had known her forever, and she smiled, a wistful look filling her eyes.

"Is she all right?" Cory asked, nodding toward the crown princess.

"Yes," Ari replied. "In this particular blood line, only sons have been born for so long nobody actually remembers a daughter born to a crown prince. Ishlie said she loves her daughters-in-law so much, but she wishes she had a daughter of her own."

"I bet Jane would be willing to give at least one up once they hit their teens," Cory snickered making them both laugh.

Turning to them, Ishlie's face was once again filled with happiness. "The procession is about to start, Ari. I suggest Abigail and your sister Cory go down the stairs where Laylin is waiting to show them to their seats. Then, you and the girls will need to come down and get ready."

"Thanks, Ishlie."

Smiling, she nodded and left the room swiftly.

"I guess Mom decided not to come?" Ari said, trying to mask her sadness. Three times in the last year, she had contacted Destra to get her to come visit, but each time she had received a reply letting her know her mother was just too busy. She would have gone to her, but Terrian had refused to allow her to leave the planet until she was fully protected.

"My daughter is unfortunately a very selfish woman," Abigail sighed. "I do believe Vane is here as he wants to see his child married. Of the two, he is much easier to get along with."

Snorting, Cory nodded. "Yeah, Vane's a kick. All right, let's go so Ari can finish getting ready to become Mrs. Terrian…" She paused and turned. "What will your last name be?"

Fidgeting a little, she shook her head in embarrassment. "I won't have a last name after this. Instead I will be…" She paused as she knew her sister would get a kick out of this. "Lady Arwen."

A laugh burst from her sister. "Ooh, Jane is going to drool on that one. Hey girls," she called to their nieces. "After today, your auntie is going to be a princess. You will have to call her Lady Auntie Ari from now on."

"Cory," she said, shaking her head in amusement.

"Ooh, Princess Ari!" Nell squealed, clapping her hands. "Our auntie is marrying a prince!"

Laughing, Cory took a couple pictures of her and the girls before she and Abigail left. Ari's nieces chattered to her and to each other for the half hour it took before they were ushered downstairs. Her heart beat fast, and she almost felt as though she would hyperventilate. Ishlie had invited over a thousand people from many different dimensions to the wedding. Ari was sure she had never met that many people in her lifetime and yet her mother-in-law informed her it was a small percentage of the people she wished to invite.

When the large wooden doors in front of her opened, she froze. Thankfully her time wasn't here yet, and all she had to do was watch each of her nieces walk forward, each one of them trying to be as dainty as possible as a maid handed them the small baskets they would carry down the aisle.

"Nervous?"

Gasping she turned and rolled her eyes at Mayir. Abigail was right. His clothing was bizarre. The only thing that came to mind when she looked at it was Robin Hood.

"Pardon?" he asked, but she just shook her head.

She could laugh at him later. The plume in the hat itself was worth at least fifty good jokes. For now, she needed to figure out how to calm herself. "There are over a thousand people in there," she hissed. "How can I walk past them all?"

He gazed over at the door and then around. "Have you nobody to walk you down the aisle?"

Embarrassed she shook her head. "No. Terrian's dad couldn't because he officiates part of the ceremony. I didn't know Vane would be here until a few minutes ago, and I don't even really know him."

"Well then," he said pompously as he held out his arm. "Might I escort you down the aisle to Lord Terrian, Lady Arwen?"

All thoughts of making fun of his outfit left her head as she realized he was the closest thing she would find to a father. As her mentor for those short few weeks, he made more of an impression on her than she could have imagined and knowing he was actually her grandfather made everything just fit. The smile started out small, but finally it spread across her face. Placing her hand in the crook of his elbow, she nodded. "I would like that, yes."

The aisle was so long she couldn't even see the people at the end of it when the doors opened. If Mayir was not holding on to her hand, she wasn't sure if she could make it to the end. After fifteen minutes of walking, she finally saw him. Standing at the end of the aisle, in front of his father, Terrian was striking in silver trousers and a silver jacket with a golden sash over his right shoulder. A few medals decorated the front of his jacket. His dark hair was pulled back at the nape of his neck, and Ari found herself staring into his bright silver eyes.

The last fifteen minutes of walking seemed instantaneous to her when all she could see was him. She was aware of him taking her hands and of turning to face him. She was also aware of his father speaking beside them, but those were only mere fragments of images in her mind. Instead, all she really saw was the handsome man in front of her.

Terrian, who she had met on an online dating site.

Terrian, who loved her so intensely he gave up his own protection to keep her safe.

Terrian, the man who did everything he could to make her happy when all she really needed was him.

The ceremony was in Darinthan. While she had learned a few words of the flowery language, most of it was still foreign to her. Thankfully, Terrian and Ishlie had practiced everything she needed to say so when her part came up, she was able to repeat the words back without a stumble. When Terrian spoke his vows, it felt as if he was saying them directly into her soul and she fought the tears stinging her eyes.

Terrian placed a silver metallic necklace around her neck and a bracelet on her wrist. There were no wedding rings on Darinth. In return, she affixed a pin on the front of his jacket as well as replaced the earring in his left ear with one she had picked out for him. Blessings were spoken by both Prince Joreth and Princess Ishlie, and then finally, Terrian took her chin in both of his hands and kissed her. Cheers erupted from both sides of the aisle, and she laughed even as tears of joy dripped down her cheeks.

The rest of the evening felt like a fairy tale. Lines and lines of people came up to offer their congratulations, but she was so happy it did not feel overwhelming at all. The hardest part was when Abigail, Cory, and the triplets came up. This would be the last time she saw her nieces. It was highly doubtful Jane would allow them to travel to another dimension again. She dropped to her knees and hugged them, reminding them to be good and to hug their mother for her.

The goodbye to Cory was no less emotional. "Shh," Cory said, hugging her tight. "This isn't goodbye, little sister. I've always kind of poo-hooed the whole interdimensional thing, but now that you are here, I might have to come visit more often. Besides, have you looked at Darinthan males? Ari, they are hot!"

"Cory!" she laughed, pulling away. "Are you forgetting Brent?"

"No, but I am an Agastion. We have no idea how long I will live. I could outlive him easily. As such, be prepared in about forty years for a visit from your sister."

Abigail was warm, but brusque, which was normal for her. "Vane was here," she informed her, "but he did not want to cause issues on your wedding day. Contact him when you are back from your honeymoon. He will come visit then."

It took over four hours, but finally she and Terrian were allowed to leave. Darinthan rose petals were tossed over their heads to shouts of "K'Lei Lei!" embarrassing her. She knew the phrase wished for strong healthy offspring. Grasping her hand, he lifted her up onto the back of his mount, Abriethon, and quickly mounted behind her. Brie, as she called him much to Terrian's amusement, immediately broke into a gallop, and they headed for the small house he had chosen for their wedding night.

The ride was easy, much easier than riding a horse, as Brie's gate was fluid no matter whether he was trotting or running full out. She leaned back against Terrian, smiling when he chuckled. "Was it too much?" he asked softly in her ear.

"Not as bad as I expected," she admitted making him laugh. "Did you catch sight of Mayir?"

"He brings out that old thing every time an official event happens," he told her. "Some think he is an idiot, but I disagree. I think he does it for two reasons. The first is because he can. Can you imagine someone laughing at him to his face? Well, except for you," he added making her laugh. "The second is because he has a lot of respect for how things used to be before interdimensional shifting became common place. Mayir is a constant reminder to think first, act second. Unfortunately, most individuals do the opposite."

Leaning against her husband, she closed her eyes as the sun slowly set. The air turned cooler, and she could hear the change in the wind as they left the city behind and Brie was able to run full out. "Up ahead," he whispered into her ear and she opened her eyes. They stood on the crest of a hill overlooking a valley. With the moon at its brightest, they clearly could see the scene below them.

A small house sat right in the middle of a large meadow covered in Darinthan moon flowers. They only bloomed under a full moon and their silver leaves glistened in the light. A small light shone in one of the windows of the house. "It's so pretty."

Brie made his way down the hill. A half hour later, Terrian let him loose before they walked up to the door. The house looked odd to her, and it took a couple minutes to realize why. "This is an Earth cottage!" she exclaimed, delighted.

"But of course. I know you like our houses well enough, but I thought I would build you something from your home. When you miss Earth, you can come here and indulge in it." Grinning, she watched him pull out what appeared to be an old fashioned key and insert it into the lock. The automated click told her it was a Darinthan electronic key, but she wasn't going to mention it. As the door swung open, revealing a warm, inviting living room with a fire burning in the fireplace, she took a step forward, stopping when his arm wrapped around her chest. "Not yet. I have researched Earth customs, and it seems that on one's wedding night, the groom carries the bride across the threshold, yes?"

Blushing a little even as a bit more of her melted at her romantic husband's gestures, she nodded. Instantly, he lifted her with his arms supporting her back and legs and carried her into the room. The living room was decorated in soft taupe. A simple long sofa faced the ornate fireplace. "This is your living room," he said. "And in here is a kitchen." He chuckled as he walked in and she looked around.

"It looks like home!"

"Of course, I told you this would be your little taste of Earth. Much of the technology is ours, but they hopefully look and feel much like home." He carried her back through the living room to the one bedroom. "And this is ours," he murmured, setting her on her feet. Her eyes fell on the bed and she began to laugh. Grinning, he stood back and watched as she ran and jumped, landing flat in the middle of it. "Okay, so not everything is from Earth."

Giggling, she lifted up her head and beckoned him closer. "It's perfect." Ever since the first night they made love, she had developed a deep appreciation for Darinthan furniture, especially Terrian's bed, a huge four-poster that had something no Earth bed would ever have. Intelligence. It woke them up in the morning, lulled them to sleep at night. And the best part was that it became almost a third partner in their sensual escapades. She really loved that bed. Even though he had Earth'd out her little cottage, he understood her enough to give her an exact replica of the bed in his, now their, room.

Crawling up next to her, he leaned over her slightly. "Now, this is a new bed. It will need to be trained," he said with a glint in his eyes. "As such, I think we should do our upmost best over the next seventeen hours, until we go on our honeymoon, to put it through its paces. What do you think?"

Squealing, she attacked him, laughing as the bed bucked and rolled underneath them. As she straddled his body, her wedding dress flowing out around her, she nodded. "In fact, maybe we should stay here the whole time. I'm sure it needs a lot of training."

The sound of a rip made her jerk as she realized he was literally ripping off her dress. "Terrian! Your mother will kill me!" she squealed, trying to grab hold of his hands before he did any more damage.

He paused and looked at her in confusion before the confusion left and he burst out laughing. "A replica of the dress is already in the archives, and you can visit it anytime you want, my dearest Ari. Quite honestly, Mother would be disappointed if anything was left of this dress to salvage. She is hoping for her next grandson in eleven months."

"So…you are supposed to destroy the dress?"

"It's a Darinthan tradition. The more the dress is destroyed, the better the chance for a fruitful union."

Relieved and amused, she released his hands. "Well, then…rip away!" For the rest of her existence, she would always remember that as the night they destroyed their first bed, something the family never let them forget.

Eleven months, two days and thirteen hours later, Crown Prince Joreth and Princess Ishlie announced the birth of their two newest grandchildren, Lord Noran and Lady Celie, their very first granddaughter.

A word about the author...

Ever since she learned to read, Cynthia Kimball has been imagining stories. As soon as she learned to write, she started penning them down. A bibliophile, she enjoys many genres of books including sci-fi/fantasy, romance, erotica, non-fiction, and all things Shakespeare.

As an artist, she knows ideas can strike at any time so she carries a tiny book around to make notes on as inspiration hits.

Her last novel, *L'Amore Perfetto*, was what she called "Romance meets modern-day fairy-tale." It was the first Dating Service novel. Currently, she is working on the next Dating Service story and two young adult books.

She is just getting started releasing the wonderful books, novels, and novellas she has written. Stay tuned for more coming your way.

http://www.cynthiakimball.com